Wolf Attack

"Stay back and shoot any of them that come at you," Slocum said to Jack.

"I ain't about to just sit here and let you do the work!"

"Then do what you please," Slocum shouted as he rode around to get a better angle on the wolves. "Just stay the hell out of our way!"

He didn't ride for long before picking a spot and coming to a halt. Every second that passed without him taking a shot felt like an eternity, and men were paying with their blood. Several Apache yelped in pain while others raised their voices in sharp battle cries. Both of those sounds blended together until it was difficult to figure out which men were in need of help and which were on the offensive. Drawing a long breath, Slocum steeled his nerves so he could push through the chaos and find his shot.

JAKE LOGAN

SLOCUM
AND THE
FOOL'S ERRAND

JOVE BOOKS, NEW YORK

THE BERKLEY PUBLISHING GROUP
Published by the Penguin Group
Penguin Group (USA) Inc.
375 Hudson Street, New York, New York 10014, USA

Penguin Group (Canada), 90 Eglinton Avenue East, Suite 700, Toronto, Ontario M4P 2Y3, Canada
(a division of Pearson Penguin Canada Inc.)
Penguin Books Ltd., 80 Strand, London WC2R 0RL, England
Penguin Group Ireland, 25 St. Stephen's Green, Dublin 2, Ireland (a division of Penguin Books Ltd.)
Penguin Group (Australia), 250 Camberwell Road, Camberwell, Victoria 3124, Australia
(a division of Pearson Australia Group Pty. Ltd.)
Penguin Books India Pvt. Ltd., 11 Community Centre, Panchsheel Park, New Delhi—110 017, India
Penguin Group (NZ), 67 Apollo Drive, Rosedale, Auckland 0632, New Zealand
(a division of Pearson New Zealand Ltd.)
Penguin Books (South Africa) (Pty.) Ltd., 24 Sturdee Avenue, Rosebank, Johannesburg 2196,
South Africa

Penguin Books Ltd., Registered Offices: 80 Strand, London WC2R 0RL, England

This is a work of fiction. Names, characters, places, and incidents either are the product of the author's imagination or are used fictitiously, and any resemblance to actual persons, living or dead, business establishments, events, or locales is entirely coincidental

SLOCUM AND THE FOOL'S ERRAND

A Jove Book / published by arrangement with the author

PRINTING HISTORY
Jove edition / December 2011

Copyright © 2011 by Penguin Group (USA) Inc.
Cover illustration by Sergio Giovine.

ISBN: 978-0-515-15019-3

JOVE®

Jove Books are published by The Berkley Publishing Group,
a division of Penguin Group (USA) Inc.,
375 Hudson Street, New York, New York 10014.
JOVE® is a registered trademark of Penguin Group (USA) Inc.
The "J" design is a trademark of Penguin Group (USA) Inc.

PRINTED IN THE UNITED STATES OF AMERICA

10 9 8 7 6 5 4 3 2 1

1

Rocas Rojas was a small town situated within spitting distance of the Potrillo Mountains. On nights like this one, locals could stand on their front porch, stare at the eastern horizon, and get a look at a line of ridges marking the border into West Texas. It was a quiet town with one saloon, one hotel, two restaurants, three shops, four whores, and a single lawman. Normally, the banjo player from the Dusty Hill Saloon played loudly enough to be heard up and down Main Street. Tonight his energetic strumming had some competition in the form of gunshots that cracked through the air from the northeast.

Gwen was one of the town's whores, and she stood at a second-floor window of the saloon, pulling a shawl around her bare shoulders and wincing as a rifle shot joined the mix. She was tall, slender, and had thick, curly hair, which rustled about her neck in the stirring breeze.

"Sounds like a real fight out there," another young woman said as she stepped up to the window to stand beside

1

her. She was shorter than Gwen, with a more rounded figure and long, straight blond hair. Her cheeks were still flushed from tending to her most recent customer, and she smelled of the cheap rosewater that was used to clean away the smell of cowboys who would rather pay for her company than a bath.

Gwen barely glanced over her shoulder before replying, "It just started. You think it's those outlaws the posse was chasing?"

The blond girl listened for a few moments and nodded. "I hope so. Hate to think we've got more than one bunch of gunmen riding around so close to town. Sounds like they're getting closer."

Closing her eyes allowed Gwen to focus on what her ears were telling her. It didn't take long before she picked up on the sound of thundering hooves. "You think it's safe out here?"

"'Course it's safe," the blonde chuckled. "Honestly, sometimes you're such a worrier."

From the hallway leading into Gwen's room, a man's voice bellowed, "You in there, Caroline?"

The blond girl rolled her eyes and pursed her lips together as if to make sure she didn't accidentally make a sound to give away her position. Unfortunately, standing in front of an open window in an otherwise darkened room wasn't the best way to remain hidden. Gwen couldn't help laughing as Caroline's lips moved in a silent plea and she drew her arms tightly around her as if she could somehow soak into the wall like drops of much-needed rain.

Footsteps from the hallway stomped toward the room and stopped so the man's bulky frame could eclipse the light coming in from the rest of the saloon. "That you, Caroline?" he asked.

When the blonde held her tongue, Gwen said, "It's her, Dale."

Caroline's eyelids snapped up and her mouth gaped open in response to the off-handed betrayal.

"He would'a found you sooner or later," Gwen said with an easy smile.

Dale filled up the doorway with a build that was mostly lard spilling over his belt. Squat legs were balanced upon feet that could have fit into boots made for a large child. "That kid you just finished with wants another go-round."

"It's only been ten minutes," Caroline whined.

"I know that! So get your backside into that room before he gets enough steam to make you work for yer money."

She thought that over and shrugged. "Guess he has a point."

Gwen started to smile back at her, but was cut short when another volley of gunfire rolled in from the surrounding desert.

"You gonna be all right?" the blonde asked.

"Caroline!" Dale snapped.

She wheeled around and hissed, "Just tell that boy I'm on my way and that he should be ready for me. With any luck, he'll be about finished before I poke my nose into that room."

Dale conceded the point with a shrug and stomped his little feet back down the hall.

"You all right?" Caroline asked.

Nodding, Gwen looked outside and rubbed her arms to guard against the night's chill. "I just worry about them, is all. Those men the sheriff is after are supposed to be killers."

"Those men are from Texas, and Texas men are mostly just full of a whole lot of big talk."

"Not all of them," Gwen pointed out. "Some bad sorts come from Texas."

"But they don't come runnin' to Rocas Rojas." Patting Gwen on the shoulder, Caroline said, "I got some work to do. That boy in the other room is sweet, but he's quicker than a jackrabbit. It won't be long before I can check on you again."

"If you like, tell him I might come in to join the two of you," Gwen said. "That should make him even quicker."

"Say that a bit louder so he can hear you through the wall and I may not have to even show my face before he's done for the night. Don't keep that window open too long. It's getting cold." Caroline turned her back to the window and headed for the door. "And don't stand there if that posse gets any closer. Don't want you getting hit by a stray bullet."

"Caroline!" Dale shouted from the hall.

Like an actress putting on a role moments before stepping onstage, the blonde applied her working persona as easily as if she were slipping into a costume. Everything from the lilt of her head to the sway in her hips became sultrier and more pronounced. Her voice was even different as she said, "Keep your pants on, Dale! As for you," she added when she got closer to the door to the room where her customer waited, "get those pants off and be quick about it."

Gwen smirked as the slam of Caroline's door was followed by the scuffling of feet and a very excited voice. No doubt, the blonde wouldn't have to do much to push that young cowboy over the edge. Since everyone in the saloon seemed to be in good hands, Gwen leaned against the window and stared outside. The hooves were drawing closer and the gunshots had eased up for the moment. If not for the shouting in the distance, she might have thought that was a good thing. Although she couldn't tell what was being said, the fact that she could hear harsh voices at all from this distance told her the men in the desert weren't swapping recipes.

When the next gunshot came, she jumped. Not only was it a sharp cracking sound in the midst of an otherwise calm

night, but it was fired from much closer than she'd anticipated. The voices that followed were closer as well.

"Here they come!" a man shouted from the corner just
a few storefronts away from the saloon. "Looks like Mark
found 'em all right!"

"I ain't deaf, you damn fool," another man snarled. "Anyone with ears can tell he didn't just stumble on some coyotes
out there."

The squabbling pair stood on the corner of Main and
Second Streets. Gwen only needed to hear their voices to
recognize them as two of the men who liked to call themselves deputies even though they weren't officially on any
payroll. Stan owned part of the dry goods store, and Oscar
rented horses out of a livery on the other side of town. Both
liked to strut about wearing their guns as if they were real
lawmen. Gwen couldn't help scowling down at the two
bumbling shapes as they hopped anxiously while the real
posse chased armed fugitives at the risk of their own lives.

"They're headed this way!" Oscar said. "Here they come.
Here they come!"

"Shut yer damn mouth or they'll know we're—"

Two horses rounded the corner as if they'd been dropped
from thin air. Between the rumble of hooves in the distance,
the usual commotion inside the saloon, and the two morons
arguing outside, Gwen hadn't heard the approach of the
two closest animals until they were barreling down Main
Street. She couldn't see much since Stan was also the one
in charge of lighting the lanterns along Main and had obviously been too preoccupied by jumping out of the street
like a frog with a firecracker stuffed up its ass to fulfill that
duty. The men on those horses kept their bodies hunkered
down low over their animals' necks, gripping their reins
tightly. Gwen took half a step away from the window until
she was fairly certain she couldn't be seen from the street
below. The entire saloon held its breath. Once the riders had
rushed past, the banjo player commenced with his song, the

rowdies downstairs commenced shouting, and the kid in the next room got the bed knocking against the wall.

"They're headed for my store!" Stan wailed as he fired a wild shot at the riders.

A few seconds later, the knocking against the wall stopped and the door to that room was opened.

After making her way into Gwen's room, Caroline said, "I got high hopes for that boy. Held out for longer than I thought this time around. What's Stan going on about down there?"

Before Gwen could answer, the rest of the hooves that had been approaching town finally reached their destination. The two would-be deputies didn't have any time to squawk before being forced against the nearest building. Three men on horseback bolted from the darkness, followed by another pair that was hot on their heels and firing at their backs. When she pulled in a breath and leaned forward to get a better look, Gwen was almost shoved out the window by the overanxious blonde.

"Is that Mark and that other fella?" Caroline asked.

"Looks that way. I better go check."

Gwen rushed from her room with Caroline following her. As the two women hurried down the stairs leading to the main floor, they created almost as much commotion as the horses that had just blazed a trail down Main Street. Dale stood at his post behind the bar, still out of breath from his trip down those same steps a few minutes ago. "Git yer asses back up them stairs, for Christ's sake!" he groused.

Gwen and Caroline ignored him, which wasn't anything new to the fat man. Rather than spend the effort it would take to go after them, he waved an exasperated hand at the women and dove back into the conversation he'd been having with one of the saloon's regular customers.

As soon as she'd shoved through the front doors, Gwen looked up Main Street to find the cloud of dust that had been kicked up by all those horses. It swirled in the cool night air as the rumbling hoofbeats rolled through town like a storm.

"You ladies shouldn't be out here," Oscar said as he stepped up to the saloon. "Dangerous sorts are about." He was a heavyset man, but had a build closer to an old stove as opposed to the large pumpkin shape of the fellow behind the Dusty Hill's bar.

Stan stood across the street, reluctant to leave the shadow that wrapped nicely around his spindly scarecrow frame.

"I saw five of them plus the posse," Gwen said. "Is that the entire gang?"

"We heard tell there was six or seven of 'em riding hard out of Texas," Oscar replied, taking a tone he saved for when he wanted to sound like an official lawman instead of a glorified errand boy. "Looks like the sheriff and that other fella dropped two of 'em outside of town."

Gwen let out a relieved breath, which was immediately drawn back in again when Oscar tacked something on to his statement.

"Either that," he said, "or them other killers are circling around town to meet up with the rest. Could be an ambush."

"Ambush?" Stan shouted from across the street. "Did you say ambush?"

"Could be."

"What?"

"I said *could be* an ambush!" Oscar hollered. Waving toward the saloon, he said, "You ladies go on inside, and I'll stop by to let you know any news I get regarding that posse." Since he figured his job was done, he ambled across the street to resume his pointless conversation with Stan.

"Oh, for heaven's sake," Gwen muttered as she ran to the corner where the dust had yet to settle.

Knowing that neither of the two men would even take notice, Caroline hurried to catch up. Both women had rounded the corner and were once again in sight of the horses before the blonde got close enough to say anything without having to shout at her friend's back. Breathing hard enough to form a cloud of steam in front of her, she asked, "What do you intend on doing out here, Gwendolyn?"

Much like a child hearing her whole name spoken by an angry parent, Gwen stopped short and focused on the source of the sternly worded question. "I have to see if he's all right."

"The only thing you'd be doing right now is getting in the way."

Unable to counter such simple logic, Gwen came to a stop. She'd lived in Rocas Rojas for so long that she could tell where she was by the texture of the boardwalk under her feet. It was a cold night and getting colder by the second, but that still wasn't enough to make her turn around and head back to the saloon.

"Come on," Carline said while wrapping a gentle yet insistent hand around Gwen's elbow. "Let's get back inside and wait for things to die down. If the sheriff hasn't raced away from here again in an hour, we can go and see what happened."

"We know what happened. A bunch of killers were chased out of West Texas and now they're here. How can you feel so calm about that?"

"Wouldn't be the first time some gunmen came here from Texas or Mexico. Remember those three fellas last spring? Or maybe you'd just remember the one with the beard and the big arms?"

"Don't try to distract me, Caroline."

Tugging on Gwen's arm, the blonde was just starting to make progress in steering her toward the saloon when shouting erupted from the direction of the sheriff's office. The little building was at the end of Third Street, which, owing to the lack of any lanterns being lit along the street, was encased in shadows thick enough to make it seem as if that section of town had been washed away in a puddle of

thick black ink. Two horses staggered awkwardly from behind that building as their riders jerked on the reins to force
the animals to step backward while turning to point their
noses in another direction.

Gwen placed her hands over her mouth, afraid that the
slightest sound might draw the wrong man's attention toward her. Whoever was fighting those horses to turn around
was also shouting obscenities at the top of their lungs before finally pulling triggers that illuminated their faces in a
flash of exploding gunpowder.

Caroline's grip tightened around Gwen's arm as she
said, "We have to get away from here!"

"No. I have to see."

"What do you want to see?"

"I have to see if—"

One of the riders got his horse facing the saloon so he
turned to look that way as well. The instant he did, he locked
eyes with Gwen.

She could feel him staring at her as if his gaze were another, even stronger, grip around her limbs that was powerful enough to root her to the spot. The second rider had
gotten his horse turned around, and both rode away from
the sheriff's office toward Gwen and Caroline.

"Bring them along with us," the first man said. He was
tall and wrapped up in what looked to be a long blue coat
that was issued by the Federal Army. The gun in his hand
may have come from the same place, but his partner
didn't look nearly as official. That one looked as if he'd
been chewed up and spit out after drying in the hot sun
for six weeks. He glared down at Gwen but, like most of
the rough types who drifted through Rocas Rojas, was
quickly distracted by Caroline. "What do you want them
fer?"

Even as gunshots blasted through the air around the far-
thest corner, the man in the Army coat barely seemed to
notice. "They'd make for fine hostages."

"As well as some comfort when we get down to Old Mex," the rougher of the two men said.

"Indeed."

With that, the rough man climbed down from his saddle while the first one shifted around to fire a few shots at the sheriff's office. The commotion in that direction was heating up even more, causing the rough man to move quicker than a flash as he lunged for Caroline.

The blonde shared a fleeting glance with Gwen, which was all either woman needed to decide what to do next. Both of them turned away from the gunmen and started running down the boardwalk. With every step, Gwen was certain she was about to get shot. After the bullet went through her, Caroline would either be chased down by the man on foot or scooped up by the one still on horseback. After that, she didn't want to think what would happen.

"Down!"

That one word sounded like a chorus of angels to Gwen, who immediately recognized the voice that had spoken it. Without hesitation, she threw herself sideways so she could tackle Caroline while following through on the simple command. Before the two women had completed their fall, another volley of gunshots filled the air.

Unlike the shots that had come before, these were strung together in quick succession and taken without concern for conserving ammunition. Lead whipped through the air amid a series of shouts and eventually pained screams as some of the rounds found their mark. Caroline twisted around to get a look at what was happening and was just in time to see the rough man's horse rearing up. She curled into a protective ball, waiting to feel powerful hooves trample her but knowing there wasn't much of anything she could do to prevent it.

One more shot hissed overhead, cutting the horse's panicked whinny short. Its hooves thumped down against the side of the boardwalk less than a foot away from Gwen's leg. After that, things got quiet.

Men's voices came from nearby, but the blood was rush-ing too quickly through Gwen's head for her to make out any words.

Spurs jangled in the street and a scuffle ensued.

More steps knocked against the boardwalk and came to a stop beside Caroline. When she shifted to look in that direc-tion, Gwen saw the face she'd been looking for the entire time.

"That was a bit closer than I'd hoped," Slocum said as he leaned down to offer a hand to her. His rough face was covered in trail dust and some blood, but was even hand-somer than she'd remembered.

Gwen took his hand and was pulled to her feet. He would have offered his other hand to Caroline, but that one was still clenched around a smoking Schofield revolver. The pistol was pointed in the general direction of the clos-est horse, which was shaking its head furiously and bucking in the middle of the street.

"You didn't shoot that horse?" Caroline asked.

"Hell no, I didn't," Slocum replied as he hauled her up. "Just put a bullet close enough to whisper into its ear and point it away from you. Now those two," he said while aim-ing at the nearby gunmen, "won't get that courtesy."

The rougher of the gunmen sat with his back against a hitching post, clutching his upper right arm with blood seep-ing through his fingers. The man in the Army coat was bleeding as well, but still in his saddle. A small wound in his leg glistened in the moonlight, but he ignored it while sitting up straight with his hands held high.

"It's all over for you," Slocum announced. "Climb down from that horse, Bill."

"I already tossed my gun," the man in the Army coat said. "But it seems fitting you'd take down an unarmed man."

The sheriff rounded the corner, holding a gun in each hand. "You killed three men in West Texas," he said while covering the outlaws. "Whatever happens to you or the ass-holes who rode with you from then on was plenty justified."

"What about the rest of my boys down the street?" Bill asked.

Without glancing around the corner to the spot where all the commotion had been, the sheriff replied, "Two are dead. The other one surrendered."

"Is he wounded?"

"Nope," the lawman said with half a smirk. "Gave up real quick once you and this other one bolted."

"Oh, fer Christ's sake," the man in the Army coat grunted. He started climbing down from his saddle, and when the sheriff stepped forward to offer some help, he refused it with a few wild swats.

2

Gwen and Caroline both hugged Slocum and were so excited they even started hopping up and down. He protested gently at first, but had to eventually force them away while wearing a pained wince.

"What's the matter?" Gwen asked. "Are you hurt? Oh my lord," she said once she saw the way he favored his left arm. "You are hurt!"

"It's nothing," he said. "Just a flesh wound."

"What happened?"

"What do you think happened? One of those assholes shot me!"

"Next time I'll fire the shot myself," the man in the Army coat said as he was shoved toward the sheriff's office. "Then you won't be around to grouse about it!"

Caroline scowled at him as well as the other two that were being led away. One was in shackles and had been collected from around the corner where the gunmen had made their initial stand. He was taken into the office, but the rough gunman who'd taken a run at the ladies was being led down the street by Oscar and Stan. "Where's he going?" she asked.

"I've been told a doctor lives down that way," Slocum said. "He's going to be stitched up and then tossed into a cage with the rest of 'em."

Gwen reached out to rub his arm, but settled for gently touching his chest. "That's where you should go, John."

"A cage?"

She smacked his chest as she replied, "No! The doctor. How bad is your arm?"

"Not bad, but the ride in didn't do it any favors."

"Is that blood?"

He looked down as if to dismiss the wound, but spotted the crimson stain soaking through the sleeve of his jacket. "Or maybe I should go to have a word with him."

"Good," Caroline said, "because I don't think those two will get him more than a few more paces before he gets away."

Slocum watched the pair of unofficial deputies try to herd the wounded man toward a narrow set of stairs leading up to the second floor of a skinny building. Even though the gunman's hands were tied behind his back by a rope that was held like a leash by Oscar and his gun belt was draped over Stan's shoulder, the outlaw was still giving his captors a fair amount of grief.

"I suppose you're right," Slocum said. "You ladies didn't get hurt yourselves, did you?"

"No, John," Gwen told him. "Get taken care of and then come tell me about what happened. You know where to find me."

"I sure do."

With that, the women walked back to the saloon while Slocum hurried to catch up to the would-be deputies. Stan barely seemed to notice when the gun belt was taken from him until after Slocum was easing it over his own shoulder. The skinny store owner wheeled around and sputtered, "Oh, it's you, Mr. Slocum. You should announce yourself before sneaking up on an armed man like that."

"You're armed?"

Stan's hand dropped to his hip where a rusted .38 hung in a holster that was obviously meant for a much bigger weapon. "Hardly seems warranted to point a gun at a wounded man."

"That wounded man would kill you in a second with his bare hands the moment he wriggled out of that rope."

When Stan saw the gunman's wrists were actually finding some room, he jumped back. "I suppose it's better to be safe than sorry."

"That's the spirit. Why don't you two go see the sheriff? I'm sure he could use some help wrangling these men's horses or getting the others settled in jail."

That was all the prompting either of the other two needed to get them to hand over the rope and rush across the street. Slocum let the leash dangle and instead gripped the section of rope that had been wrapped around the gunman's wrists. Tightening his grip until the rope dug into the other man's flesh, he shoved the outlaw into the wall directly beside the foot of the stairs. "Sorry about that, Ed. Guess my balance is off after all that riding."

"Then how about you take a load off, Slocum? I can find my own way."

"Wouldn't think of it. Up you go."

Slocum shoved the outlaw hard enough to make sure it was a genuine struggle for him to get to the second floor without breaking his neck. By the time they got to the door at the top of the stairs, the outlaw was winded and fighting even harder to free himself.

"I'll see to it that you die for killing my friends," Ed snarled.

"You mean the friends that killed all those innocent folks who were riding in stagecoaches to visit family and such when they were robbed? Or the friends that killed those people in them banks?" When Ed tried to respond to that, Slocum shoved him hard enough to knock the outlaw's head against the door. "Sorry. What was that?"

Ed was stupid enough to try speaking again, so Slocum knocked his head against the door one more time.

Suddenly, the door was pulled open by a man wearing a long nightshirt and a tattered quilt wrapped around him like a shawl. He had a beak-like nose, sunken features, and a scalp that was bald apart from a thin band of hair running from the back of one ear and around to the back of the other. Although he was annoyed at first, his expression shifted quickly when he saw what had been used to rattle his door on its hinges.

"Sorry to wake you, Doc," Slocum said. "But I've got a customer for you."

Collecting himself, the man wrapped in the blanket said, "I presume this is in relation to all the noise from a few minutes ago?"

"You'd presume correctly. He's been shot."

The doctor's eyes were drawn immediately to Ed's shirt, which was a disheveled mess. After pulling it open to get a look at the outlaw's wound, he said, "Better bring him in."

Slocum shoved Ed into the modest dwelling, kicked the door shut behind him, and then pushed him until the outlaw was tripped up by a cot set up against one wall. Ed dropped down amid a string of obscenities that didn't let up until Slocum was through tying the other end of the rope to the cot's frame. Ed tested the rope with a few tugs, which only cinched the knot around his wrists even tighter.

"Is that necessary?" the doctor asked while pointing at the rope.

"You heard the shooting, right?" Slocum asked. "You think he's got it all out of his system?"

When the doctor saw the feral glint in the outlaw's eye, his concern for the gunman's comfort was no longer such a pressing matter. "I see some blood on your jacket as well. Are you hurt?"

"It's just a nick."

"Let me have a look."

Slocum peeled off his jacket and rolled up his sleeve to show the doctor a blood-soaked bandanna tied around his arm. Beneath the bandanna was a patch of rough skin held together by a jagged line of thick black thread. "Did the stitches myself," Slocum said.

"Seeing that you would have only been able to use one hand, I suppose that explains why it looks like you were pieced together like a bad pair of shoes."

"And since we rousted you from your bed at such a late hour, I suppose that explains why you're being such a snippy little prick."

The doctor sighed and shrugged out of his quilt in favor of a proper robe. "Will there be any more wounds for me to tend this evening? If need be, I can find my way to Sheriff Reyes's office."

"No need for that. Just us two and one with a scratch at the sheriff's office. How about you tend to me first?"

"This man looks like he has a more serious injury," the doctor said as he looked over at Ed. The outlaw smiled back at Slocum as if he'd just won a prize.

Slocum pulled up a chair and made himself comfortable. "Sounds fair enough. I'll just sit here and make sure he doesn't step out of line. And just so I know in case he does decide to be difficult, where might I find the undertaker?"

That question, spoken without the first hint of humor or leverage, drained all of the color from Ed's face as well as a good portion of what was in the doctor's. Not knowing how else to respond, the doctor said, "That'd . . . umm . . . that'd be just down the street."

"Much obliged, Doc. You may commence."

After that, Ed was no longer in the mood to struggle or

even speak as the doctor set about the task of cleaning and tending to the outlaw's wound. It was a messy gash in his arm that was still blackened from the passage of the bullet.

"So," the doctor said after he'd fallen into a rhythm of well-practiced motions, "may I ask what caused this trouble?"

"You hear of a man named Oklahoma Bill Dressel?" Slocum asked.

"The stagecoach robber from Texas?"

"That's the one. He and his boys robbed a few little banks in some towns that nobody's ever heard of. Might have gotten away with it, too, if they just would've slunk away quietly like the snakes they are. Instead," Slocum added while banging his foot against Ed's cot, "they decided to try and ransom a hostage taken from one of the stagecoaches. Some pretty girl with a rich daddy who put up a reward for her capture."

"So you were after the reward?"

"Not as such. Your sheriff got some information about where the gang might be hiding. He didn't have a lot to pay for a posse, but I signed on for a percentage of the reward that'll be coming for the gang's capture. Funny thing is that nobody seems to know about the price on Ed's scalp."

Even though the doctor's hand hadn't wavered as he expertly tended to the wound, the outlaw flinched.

"Seems ol' Ed raped a few other girls back East," Slocum said. "He's got a taste for the ones with yellow hair and prosperous families. Well, prosperous enough to scrape together a reward for his worthless hide. After spending this bit of time with him, I think I may just hand him over for free." Before the outlaw could put on any kind of smug expression, Slocum added, "Just as long as I get to be there when all six of that poor girl's brothers ride all the way out from Boston just to beat you to a pulp."

"Rapist, huh?"

"That's right, Doc."

"Well then," the doctor said as he applied a bandage with just a bit too much enthusiasm, "perhaps I can tend to you now after all. You've probably got things to do and this one won't be very busy for a while."

"Much obliged."

As much as Slocum wanted to head straight to the Dusty Hill Saloon, there was still some business to tend to. The first task was to tie Ed's wrists in a more secure knot as well as bind his ankles so he couldn't do much more than grunt through the bandanna that had been stuffed into his mouth. After that, he made certain the remaining outlaws had been tossed into the jail at the back of the sheriff's office. The two men in the cell still had some steam in their engines, but that didn't last long after Slocum arrived.

"Where's Ed?" the leader of the outlaws asked. Although he no longer wore his Army coat, he still carried himself as if he had an official rank and was entitled to all the privileges thereof.

"Doc's stitching him up," Slocum replied.

The sheriff had a round face and coal black hair. Several days' worth of whiskers sprouted from his chin, which made him look even more tired as he said, "Guess I should go over there to keep an eye on him."

"I wrapped him up pretty good, but sitting with him may not a bad idea." When he saw the tired look on the lawman's face, Slocum said, "On second thought, why don't I head back over there?"

"Naw, I can go. You've done plenty already, John."

"It wasn't for free. I'm still getting a cut of that reward money, right?"

"Sure," the lawman said. "It's the least I can do."

"The least you can do is buy me a steak dinner."

"A bucket of slop's all you deserve," the gang leader said from within the cell.

The sheriff silenced him with a swift kick to one of the

bars. "I'm part owner of the Dusty Hill. Dale cooks a fine slab of beef. You can eat there free of charge. How'd that be?"

"Now that's right neighborly of you, Mark," Slocum said. "How about a bottle of whiskey to go along with that steak?"

"Don't push it."

Slocum conceded the point and strode out of the office. By the time he got back to the doctor's room on the second floor of the building across the street, Ed was patched up and lying still upon the cot.

"Passed out," the doctor said by way of an explanation.

"He ready to be moved?"

"It'd be good for him to rest for a day or two. Although I'm a little leery about leaving him here."

"Figured you might be," Slocum said before showing the doctor the handcuffs and leg irons he'd brought over from the sheriff's office. Once those were in place, the doctor was finally able to let go of the breath he'd been holding. Ed, on the other hand, was barely able to draw a gulp of air as he was shaken awake and forced outside, down the street, and into the sheriff's jail.

From there, Slocum walked over to the Dusty Hill Saloon farther down on Main Street. The barkeep tossed him a quick wave and shouted, "Appreciate the show, Mr. Slocum!"

"And I'd appreciate a drink."

A small glass of whiskey was poured in front of him, which Slocum downed in one swallow. The firewater did a nice job of cutting through the grit that had collected in his throat after several days of hard riding. Normally, he would have taken another drink to ensure a good night's sleep, but he doubted he would need any help in that regard.

"Got any scalps to hang on the wall?" Dale asked from where he sat beside the barkeep.

"Better ask the sheriff. I'm about to fall over."

Tossing a key to him, Dale said, "Your room's right where you left it."

Slocum trudged up the stairs, walked down the hall to the second door on the left, and fit his key into the lock. The room was dark and quiet. The shades were drawn, but as soon as his eyes adjusted to the shadows, he picked out something other than the pile of blankets on his bed.

"What took you so long?" Gwen asked in a soft, purring voice.

Slocum stripped out of his clothes, piling everything on top of his boots in a heap before setting his gun belt within easy reach of the bed. "If your sheriff hired some real deputies, I would've been back a lot sooner."

He crawled under the blankets, stretched out his legs, and soon felt Gwen's hands slide across his chest. He couldn't see much more than the shape of her beside him, but could feel the smooth, warm contours of her naked body brushing against his leg and side.

"I was worried about you," she whispered.

Although his body began to respond to her, he barely had enough wind in his sails to say, "No need to worry."

She said something else, but her words were lost when Slocum inadvertently dropped into a deep, all-encompassing sleep.

3

Slocum woke up just enough to feel the outside world again. More specifically, he felt the warmth of his blankets as well as the body beside him. The moment he stirred, Gwen shifted as well.

"Good morning," she whispered.

Sunlight scraped at the edges of the blinds, casting the room in a dim, dusty glow. "Feel like I could sleep for the whole day."

"You wouldn't want to do that."

"Why not?" he asked.

Gwen's only response was to slip her hand between his legs so she could rub his inner thigh before cupping him in a gentle hold. Her fingers massaged him, and he quickly became hard enough for her to start stroking his growing length.

"Oh," he said. "That's why not."

"You want me to let you sleep?"

Slocum blinked away some of the weariness and shifted onto his side so he could look at her face while allowing her hand to reach him even easier. She took advantage right

away and began stroking his growing erection more vigorously. "I could use some sleep," he said, "but maybe I could
use something else a bit more."

"Really? If you need to sleep so badly, I could always let
you get back to it."

"Too late for that," he said while pulling her closer. "Now
you've got to finish what you started."

Gwen laughed softly and draped a leg over him. She lay
on her side as well, which allowed their bodies to entwine
perfectly. Her breasts were just large enough to fill his hand,
and her large nipples were already erect. She always liked it
when he touched her that way, and this time was no excep-
tion. The more Slocum massaged her breast, the harder she
stroked him. Finally, he was rigid enough for him to feel a
yearning ache throughout the entire lower half of his body.

Although she stopped stroking him, she didn't let go.
Gwen guided Slocum's rigid pole until he could feel it
touch the damp patch of downy hair between her legs. The
tip of his cock slipped between the lips of her pussy, stok-
ing the fire inside them both. When he shifted his hips, he
eased in just a little bit more. He stayed there while kissing
her hard on the mouth. As he moved back and forth within
her, Gwen moaned softly and began scraping her nails
against Slocum's shoulders. Her tongue slipped into his
mouth, and her entire body trembled with anticipation. He
could only tolerate that for another couple of seconds before rolling Gwen onto her back so he could climb on top
of her.

She spread her legs open wide for him, placing her
hands on his arms and gazing up expectantly as he reached
down to guide his cock back into her. The instant his hard
member found the warmth between her glistening lips,
Slocum pushed his hips forward and drove into her so they
could both let out grateful breaths.

Slocum's first few movements were slow and steady.
She was so wet and ready for him that he glided in and out

of her with ease. When he buried himself in as far as he could go, he held there and kissed her some more. That way, when he ground his hips between her thighs, he could feel her moan rush directly into his mouth. As soon as he rose above her, Gwen turned her head and clenched her eyes tightly shut. He pumped vigorously into her, giving in completely to what he'd been craving from the instant he felt her smooth, warm body beside him.

Gwen's hips moved in time to his rhythm. Every time he entered her, she let out a short, urgent breath.

Slocum's chest was raised just enough for him to feel her nipples brushing against it. He reached down to cup her again while straightening up so he was on his knees between her legs. That way, he could look down at her writhing, naked body as she reached down to hastily guide him back into her.

"Don't stop, John," she sighed. "I need you inside me."

He closed his eyes and savored the touch of her hand against his erection. When he felt that he was inside her again, Slocum grabbed her legs and positioned them so they rested upon his shoulders when he resumed thrusting to bury his cock even deeper into her. Gwen started to say something, but her words came out as nothing more than breathy moans. She reached up to grab the headboard and moaned louder every time his body pounded against hers.

As he drove into her, Slocum ran his hands up and down along Gwen's legs. Her muscles were taut beneath her skin, and she writhed slowly in response to his every move. When he reached all the way down to cup her backside, he was able to pull her up a bit as he thrust forward. It didn't take much more to drive her to the breaking point. Gwen bit down on her lower lip as her pussy tightened around him. Slocum drove into her hard and deep until she was shuddering with pleasure.

It was a sight to behold. The entire front of her body glistened with sweat. Her breasts stood proudly, beckoning to him, so Slocum cupped them in both hands. He massaged the supple flesh while pumping into her as hard or soft as he pleased. After her climax, Gwen opened her eyes and watched him intently. She barely seemed to have the strength to move, but reached up to hold on to his arms. Slocum kept his hands on her breasts, feeling their weight in his grasp as he pumped vigorously in and out of her. The fire in him grew and his blood rushed through his veins, speeding him to the inevitable conclusion.

He pounded into her once more before exploding inside her. For a moment, he felt as if he had enough energy to charge outside and run all the way to the Canadian border. About two seconds after that, it was all he could do to steer himself to one side before collapsing on top of her.

Once Slocum had hit the mattress and rolled onto his back, Gwen curled up beside him to drape a leg across his waist and an arm over his chest. "Now that," she sighed, "was worth waiting for."

"Yes," Slocum breathed. "Yes, it was."

"Are you all right?"

"A little winded, but fine."

"Are you sure?"

"All right," he admitted. "Maybe more than a little winded. Just need to catch my breath, is all."

Gwen's voice took a more serious tone as she propped herself up and said, "That's not what I meant. You're bleeding!"

Slocum's eyes snapped open. Sure enough, the fingers she showed him were smeared with a thin layer of blood. "What the hell?"

Fidgeting until she could get herself upright with her legs tucked beneath the rest of her body, Gwen allowed the covers to fall away from her so she could look down at him. "I think you're cut."

"Well, you did scratch me pretty good there," Slocum chuckled.

Gwen swung herself around and climbed out of bed. Hurrying across the room, she tugged at the shade to expose just enough of the window for a healthier dose of sunlight to enter. Not only did that illuminate the room, but it allowed Slocum to see the smooth contours of her naked body as she rushed back to climb onto the bed. "Yes," she said. "You're cut. It's your arm."

Feeling his body responding to the sight of her, Slocum reached out to pull her closer while saying, "It's fine. Wanna scratch me up some more?"

"No, John! This is serious."

"Done with me already? I must be losing my touch."

Gwen looked down at him like a stern schoolmarm. Taking firm hold of his left wrist, she pulled his arm up sharply enough to send a jolt of pain through that entire side.

"Ow, dammit!" he snarled.

"See?" she said while shaking her head. "I told you it was serious. Now will you pay attention?"

Slocum wrangled free of her grip while sitting up so his back was against the headboard. Once he was situated, he looked down at his left arm to find it covered in an irregular coat of blood. It seeped from the wound he'd gotten while riding with Sheriff Reyes and had even soaked into a nasty-looking stain on the sheets. "Aw hell. Tore my damn stitches."

"How did that happen?"

"Yeah," Slocum said in an impatient tone. "I wonder how that might have happened."

She propped her hands on her knees and tried to maintain her stern demeanor. Seeing as how she was still naked and framed in a hazy glow of sunlight, it would have been difficult for her to look anything close to what she was aiming for. "You have a smart mouth, John Slocum. Try not to talk that way to Doc Bower when you see him about fixing those stitches."

"Is that his name?"

"Yes," she replied while climbing out of bed once again so she could start gathering his clothes. "I would think you'd know that after all the time you spent with him last night."

"I spent more time tying a man down like a dog. Besides, I don't need to see the doctor again. I can stitch myself just fine."

"Really? Is that why the doctor had to do the job again for you?"

Slocum studied his arm as the other man's evaluation of his stitching drifted through his mind. Although he thought he'd done a better job than the doctor had given him credit for, it was no picnic doing it himself. The first time had been out of necessity. Doing so again would only be an exercise in bullheadedness. "Fine," he said while pulling on his jeans. "I'll go, but only because you asked so nicely."

"I need you stitched up properly," she said while helping him into his shirt and buttoning it. "That way you can withstand another night here with me."

"Another night, huh?"

She shrugged before smirking and adding, "Or afternoon. Depends on how quickly you get to Doc Bower's."

That was all the inspiration he needed to pull on the rest of his clothes, buckle his gun belt around his waist, and head for the door.

"What on earth have you been doing?" Doc Bower asked as he examined Slocum's arm. "Wrestling wild animals?"

"Not exactly."

Judging by the way he groused at Slocum, the doctor had a good idea of what had caused the tear and didn't approve one bit. "At least you didn't try to patch it together yourself this time."

"Yeah, Doc. I much prefer the warmth of your company."

Bower held him at arm's length and stared at him through a pair of little round spectacles perched upon the edge of his nose. Before too long, his sunken face broke into a wide grin that seemed like it would have been more befitting a patient who hadn't survived one of his procedures. "Fair enough. Let me get my things."

Slocum sat in a large dentist's chair in the main room of the doctor's office. The spot where he'd been stitched up the night before was one floor directly above. Having collected a needle, thread, and smock to wear over his shirt and tie, Bower looked more like a fancy butcher when he started sewing the wound shut.

The skin was tender after having already been ripped apart three times and stitched twice. If there had been any cobwebs in Slocum's head after his night's sleep followed by the morning's activities, they were banished real quickly once the needle punctured his arm.

Speaking as if he were conversing over a cup of freshly brewed tea, Bower said, "Sheriff Reyes has been in over his head lately."

"Oklahoma Bill is enough to give any lawman fits," Slocum hissed as the thread was cinched to squeeze together two flaps of skin.

Bower continued his work. To his credit, he had a smooth enough touch that Slocum might not have felt much of any discomfort if not for the tenderness of the wound. Perhaps wearing his glasses improved the doctor's performance over the previous night. "Oklahoma Bill. Sounds like one of those names the newspapers latch on to. I prefer to not get wrapped up in all the dramatics of such unfortunate events."

"Men like Bill are fond of dramatics. They're also fond of burning through broken trails and shooting anything that tries to stand in their way. Shouldn't discredit any lawman who brings in someone like that. Not to mention when he also brings in the rest of the gang."

"As I was saying, Sheriff Reyes has been in over his head. Not just with this Oklahoma person, but in general."

Hearing the ham-handed way Doc Bower dealt with a

simple nickname was enough of an amusement to take Slocum's mind from the stinging needle and itchy thread.

"I don't know if you've met the two fellows who fancy themselves as deputies," Bower continued, "but they're about as useful as tits on a bull."

Not only did that sound unnatural coming from the doctor, but it was fairly obvious it had been spoken as an attempt to talk down to what he thought was Slocum's level. Since it was still amusing to hear, Slocum let it pass. "I met Stan and Oscar," he said. "I'd have to agree with your assessment of those two."

Bower chuckled, which was the first time his hand wavered enough for Slocum to feel it. "The sheriff is wise to keep them off a payroll. That would only make them lazier, if that's possible. What he needs is a real deputy. The fact that he chose you for such a dangerous job and had such great success speaks volumes of how well you'd work out in the position."

"I was here when the word came through about Bill and his men making their run out of West Texas. I've known Mark Reyes for a few years, so was glad to help when he asked. This is a fine little town and he's been doing a good job of keeping it that way. If he needed more help, he would ask for it."

"Mark's a proud man," the doctor said. "That's why he didn't ask you to stay. So I'm asking."

"Appreciate the vote of confidence, Doc, but you shouldn't let one rough night rattle you so much. Once word spreads about what happened to Bill and his boys once they got here, I doubt any gunman will be too quick to visit this town anytime soon."

Since verbal brawls were obviously his preferred arena, Bower steeled himself for another round. "Yes, but isn't it plausible that there may be friends or associates of this man from Oklahoma that remain unaccounted for?"

"I'm not even sure if he is from Oklahoma."

"Then why on earth would he attach that to his name?"

Slocum had never been so grateful to hear a piercing scream as he was when one such noise ripped down Main Street since it was loud enough to distract the doctor and end the increasingly maddening conversation. Unfortunately, whoever was doing the screaming seemed to be headed straight for Bower's office.

4

Doc Bower finished up Slocum's stitches in a rush. The job wasn't perfect and it sure as hell wasn't painless, but the wound was closed and the needle was removed from his flesh. "Here," the doctor said while tossing some bandages at him. "Since you fancy yourself a field surgeon, perhaps you could dress that arm in my stead. It seems I have another patient on the way."

"Sure thing, Doc."

Slocum wrapped the bandages around his arm, and by the time he was tying them off, the source of all that screaming staggered into the large windowed front door of the office. Not through the door. Into it. His height was difficult to determine because he was hunched over so badly, but he couldn't have been any taller than Slocum. Judging by the way he gripped the front of his body and staggered repeatedly into the door like a bird flopping into a freshly cleaned window, he seemed to have been knocked in the head. He may have been shot in the stomach, although there wasn't quite enough blood to fit that bill. When Doc Bower tried to open his office door while the wounded man repeatedly pushed it shut in his attempts to get inside, it put on a show that was amusing enough for Slocum to sit down and watch for a while.

"For heaven's sake," Bower sighed. "Step back."

"I'm hurt! Need a damn doctor!" the man outside wailed.

"I am a doctor."

"Then let me in!"

"Step back, I implore you."

"But I need to get *in*!"

Slocum couldn't help chuckling. All that was missing was a piano accompaniment.

Finally, Bower timed an attempt so he could open the door after the man outside bounced off it. For a finale, he managed to clip the man in the side of the face with the edge of the door when the bloody fellow tried to rush inside. After catching the frantic man, the doctor looked over to Slocum with a stern glare that proved he knew exactly how amused he was. Either that, or Slocum had accidentally laughed louder than he'd intended.

"You should probably get a door that opens in," Slocum offered.

"I didn't build the place," Bower snapped.

After taking a breath, the man from outside sobbed, "Yeah. Fix yer door!"

Biting back his retort to those comments, Bower asked, "What happened to you, sir?"

Now that the man was standing beside Bower, Slocum could see he was a bit shorter than the doctor, which made him a few inches shorter than him. A thick mop of tan hair was snarled with everything from dust to bits of dead leaves, and the beard covering the lower half of his face obviously hadn't been tended in weeks. Slocum wasn't the sort who normally took notice of the color of a man's eyes, but it was hard to miss the huge, cloudy green orbs embedded in this one's panicked face as he let out another wailing scream.

"Take a breath," the doctor said.

The man drew a breath and screamed again.

"You'll have to calm down, sir," Bower said.

The man hollered.

"Sir!"

Another scream.

Slocum stepped forward and swung a quick backhand that caught the screaming man in the face. It was so fast and so unexpected that it silenced the wounded fellow as well as the doctor trying to tend to him.

"Go ahead, Doc," Slocum said as he sat back down.

Still stunned by the display, Bower straightened the spectacles on his nose and said, "Yes, well, let's take a look at what we're dealing with here."

The wounded man was still simpering as Bower peeled his arms away from where they were clenched around his torso. Instead of a stomach wound or anything on his body, the source of the blood was the man's right hand. When the doctor tried to get a closer look, the man looked as if he was going to start wailing again. One quick glance in Slocum's direction nipped that idea in the bud and he choked down a shuddering breath.

"Were you shot?" Bower asked. "There's been a lot of that going around, you know."

His lame attempt at a joke didn't come close to making a dent in the wounded man's panic. Slocum was reminded of a little boy who'd cut his finger and couldn't settle down enough to get a single word out. Of course, when the man finally extended his right arm to show his hand to the doctor, it was clear that he suffered from a lot more than a cut.

"Oh my," Bower said. He stretched a hand back toward Slocum and said, "Hand me a towel, please."

It took a few seconds for Slocum to turn and find the small cabinet stocked with towels, washcloths, and bandages. By the time he picked up some linens and turned back around to hand them to the doctor, he could see even more of what had brought the man into Bower's office. The man's hand was slick with blood that covered it like a thick coat of wet paint. As far as he could tell, the only finger that was still intact was the smallest one. The other three had been ripped off to leave thin stumps of varying lengths. The thumb seemed to be all there, but was covered with too much blood for him to be certain. Slocum was no stranger to gruesome sights, but this one was enough to give him a moment's pause. As for the doctor, he became calmer as more of the grievous injury was revealed.

"I see three fingers have been partially severed," Bower said. "Can you feel this?"

When the doctor touched each stump, the man reacted as if he'd been prodded with a red-hot poker. "Hell yes, I can feel that!"

"Well, it would be worse if you couldn't feel anything in those extremities," Bower said while taking a towel from Slocum. "How long ago did the injury occur?"

The man was having trouble making more than a few unintelligible sounds. His face looked more like a chalky mask beneath several layers of dust and whiskers.

"Sir. Tell me your name."

"J . . . Jack."

"Jack?"

"Jack Halsey."

"Pleased to meet you, Mr. Halsey. I'm Dr. Bower. Take a breath and sit still while I clean this wound. John, get me some water, won't you?"

"Sure, Doc."

"You'll have to sit still, Jack, if you want me to tend to this."

"And you'll have to just do yer damn job," Jack replied. "Make sure I don't die from this hand bleedin' out and stop flappin' yer damn gums!"

"I know it hurts, but—"

Jack attempted to reach across his body with his left hand to pull the pistol from a holster strapped around his waist. That movement was enough to twist the hand in Bower's grasp, which sent another wave of pain through his entire body.

"Am I going to have to ask my friend here to restrain you?" Bower asked.

Slocum had returned with a basin of water, and Jack looked up at him as if he were staring into the face of the devil himself. Twitching in the spot where he'd been backhanded a little while ago, Jack meekly replied, "No sir."

"Good. Now sit still and let me do my job. I think it'd be prudent for you to be relieved of your weapon. John's going to take it from you and you're going to let him."

Jack did as he was told, making certain to keep his eyes on Slocum.

After lifting the gun from Jack's holster, Slocum walked over to set it on a table at the far end of the room. It was a rusted old .44, and it looked as if it had been pieced together from bits of other guns that had been left in a scrap pile. Considering the sorry state of the weapon, he would have hated to see the pieces that Jack had left behind. "What happened to your hand?" Slocum asked as he approached the doctor and his newest patient. "Were you foolish enough to pull the trigger of that piece of shit gun you're carrying?"

In short order, Bower washed away enough of the blood to get a clearer look at Jack's hand. The first two fingers had been torn off messily above the knuckle. Half of the third finger remained, and it seemed the tip of his thumb had been sheared as well. As he'd deduced earlier, the little finger was unscathed.

"I'll have you know I made that pistol!" Jack said.

"Oh, I think I figured that much out for myself."

Wringing out the bloody cloth he was using, Bower dipped it into the water and continued dabbing at Jack's hand. "How did this happen?"

"I was attacked by wolves."

Bower stopped what he was doing and waited. When no

more of an explanation seemed to be coming, he asked, "Are you joking?"

"No, I'm not joking."

Slocum leaned in to get a look at the fingers. Now that they'd been on display for so long, the sight of them wasn't nearly so unsettling. The flesh was shredded and the skin was torn. Nubs of bone protruding from the skinny stumps were splintered and jagged. "Looks about right to me."

"Well, thank you for your approval, asshole."

"Manners," Bower reminded his patient.

Since the doctor still had a hold of his savaged hand, Jack choked down whatever other foul names he had in mind for Slocum. "It was wolves," he said. When he looked down at his hand, he paled even more and forced himself to look over at the office's front window. A few locals stood there, gazing inside. Although they'd been anxious to see what had become of the man who'd run screaming down the street, the two old ladies and a man in his forties were in no hurry to stay once they caught sight of Jack's hand.

"Sure it was more than one wolf?" Slocum asked.

"What difference does that make?"

"First of all, you're in pretty good shape even if only one wolf got a hold of you. Second, now's not exactly the time for you to be lying about what happened. Save the impressive stories for the ladies."

"I'll have to agree," Bower said. "It could make a big difference if there were anything like toxic substances involved or—"

"Wolves ain't toxic enough for ya?" Jack growled.

"More than one?" Slocum asked.

Through gritted teeth, Jack replied, "Just one got me, but it was part of a pack."

Before the other two could lock horns again, Bower said, "That's good enough for me. I've got plenty of work to do and need to get to it."

"Do you need any help, Doc?"

"No!" Jack said. "That one already struck me once."

"Because you deserved it," Bower was quick to say. Jack started to slump over as he finally lost the last bit of color in his face. When he passed out, Slocum had rushed around in time to catch him.

"Where should I take him?" Slocum asked.

"To that bed over there," the doctor replied while pointing to a bed that butted against a cabinet containing what looked to be a wide array of surgical instruments.

"You got any rope?"

Thinking back to the previous night, Bower didn't so much as chuckle at the joke. "Just hold him down, if you would. I'd like to do as much work as possible while he's out, but it would only make things worse if he came to at the wrong moment."

"Sure thing."

The next few hours went by quickly and Slocum was too preoccupied to keep an accurate count of how many had passed. No matter what problem he may have had with the doctor regarding his mannerisms or conversational ability, Slocum couldn't fault the man's professional skills. Bower cleaned up Jack's hand until it was cleaner than the rest of him and then got to work on the fingers.

One by one, the roughest sections of skin were trimmed away and what remained looked less like something that had been gnawed on by a wild animal. At one point, Jack stirred. Slocum held him down, but didn't have to do that for long because the doctor took that opportunity to file down a sharp splinter of protruding bone. His movements were quick and efficient, but caused enough pain to send the wounded man back into unconsciousness.

"Almost done," Bower said.

"Good. I think I've seen enough doctoring to last me for a good, long while."

"I wouldn't have pegged you for the squeamish sort."

"Not squeamish, Doc. I've just had my fill."

Glancing over at the table where Jack's gun rested, Bower asked, "So do you think this man is dangerous?"

"I don't think you need to worry about someone who can't keep their hands out of a wolf's mouth," Slocum replied.

"He strikes me as something more than some unlucky vagrant. He is armed, after all."

"Most everyone is."

"So he strikes you as a stable man?"

"I didn't say that," Slocum clarified. "I just meant that most everybody who rides on their own from one town to another carries a gun."

"In case you haven't noticed, this town has been getting more than its share of armed visitors lately. Do you think this could be one of the men associated with that Oklahoma person?"

Slocum looked down at Jack's face. Although he wasn't seriously considering the possibility that he rode with Oklahoma Bill Dressel, he'd crossed paths with plenty of other folks that had caused more than their share of trouble. Even when he tried to imagine what Jack might look like under all that dirt, he still couldn't come up with anyone that struck a chord. Finally, he said, "Sorry, Doc. It seems like you've just got a common, run-of-the-mill lunatic with three missing fingers."

"And wolves."

"Sure."

"We could still use someone in town to lend Sheriff Reyes a hand."

"After all you've seen here in this very office, you're going to tell me that the sheriff is the one who needs a hand?"

Bower looked down at the wound he was dressing, shook his head, and started to laugh. "Thanks, John. I needed that."

5

When he stepped out of the doctor's office, Slocum had intended on letting Gwen know where he'd been before scraping up some breakfast. With the images of the finger surgery and the stench of all that blood still fresh in his nose, however, he decided on taking a walk to clear his head first. A few minutes of fresh air were all he needed, and he soon found himself back at the Dusty Hill Saloon. Gwen fussed over him for a bit before leading him to a table where Dale brought him some coffee. She disappeared for a little while and returned with biscuits and gravy.

"I thought we had sausages," she told him, "but some poker players ate the last of them after gambling for eighteen hours straight."

"Don't mention it," Slocum said. "Anything remotely looking like a finger wouldn't have set well anyhow."

"Pardon me?"

"Never mind. When does the sheriff get to his office?"

"Should be there now, I suppose. Why?"

"I've still got some money to collect."

She nodded and smiled knowingly. "You mean a reward?"

"Call it what you like. I need it."

"And I thought this might be about the man with the bloody hand."

"You know about him, huh?"

"Kind of hard not to," she replied. "He staggered in from the desert without a horse, holding his hand and crying to high heaven!"

"So if he was making such a spectacle, someone other than you must have seen him. Why didn't anyone help him get to the doctor's office?"

"He had a gun," Gwen told him while standing up to gather the dirty plates. "And he was screaming like a banshee, waving his hand and throwing blood everywhere. I never heard such cussing! He looked like a crazy man. Would you have been so quick to walk up and offer assistance?"

"I suppose not. Does he look familiar?"

She balanced the plates in one hand and propped the other on her hip. "Just because I work in this saloon, you think I'd be familiar with some lunatic who staggers in from God knows where?"

"Yes." His quick response caught her flatfooted and put a stunned expression onto her face. Before she could rip into him with a reply, he added, "You said he didn't have a horse, so that means he couldn't have walked too far on his own while bleeding so badly. Seems like he could be local, is all I meant."

"Is it, now?"

"Well, I also meant to put that funny look on your face. Couldn't help myself."

She rolled her eyes, turned away from him, and walked to the small kitchen situated just off the main saloon. She must have dumped the dishes in a pile for someone else to sort through because she reappeared before the batwing doors could stop swinging. Approaching Slocum's table, she took a seat and crossed her arms. The expression she wore was intently focused, but quickly dissolved into a shrug. "If he is local, I don't think I've seen him. Could just mean he never came into this place before. I don't see much outside these walls."

"Could be a miner or trapper," Slocum mused. "Or a hunter passing through the mountains or on his way to somewhere else. Could just be a lunatic who wandered in to scream at a town."

"All just as likely. Why so concerned?"

"I don't know," he told her. "Just a strange way to start the day." He pushed away from the table and stood up. "I'll have a word with the sheriff about my money."

"Come back to see me soon," Gwen said as she stood, grabbed his shirt, and pulled him down just enough so she could whisper directly into his ear, "I bet we could do some things that'll make you forget all about that strangeness."

"I should probably watch my stitches."

"Then lay down and let me take care of you. I'll be gentle."

"You'd better not," he said while giving her backside a firm swat. "I like your wild side."

Slocum left the saloon and walked along Main Street. In the short time it took to reach the sheriff's office, he couldn't stop thinking about one of the questions Gwen had asked. Why was he so concerned about Jack Halsey and his missing fingers? Maybe, after all of the strangeness he'd seen in his life, Slocum knew better than to just assume some of it would pass him by without further incident. Of course, that didn't mean he had to go looking for it. Rather than concern himself anymore with the crazy son of a bitch, he pushed open the sheriff's door and stepped inside.

Mark Reyes sat behind his desk with his feet propped up and his hands folded across his chest. His hat was positioned over most of his face, and he barely seemed to notice

Slocum's presence. Instead of announcing himself formally, Slocum banged a foot against the lawman's desk and let out a loud cough.

Reyes swung his feet down and reflexively reached for his gun. He had enough of his wits about him to keep from skinning the smoke wagon.

"Vigilant as ever, huh, Sheriff?" Slocum chided.

"I can still feel the damn horse beneath me, and those two good-for-nothings who hound me for deputy badges are in their homes tucked into warm beds," Reyes said while getting to his feet and stretching his back. "You're after your money?"

"That's right."

"Any way I could convince you to stay on in a more official capacity?"

"Is the pay that good?" Slocum asked.

Having reached into his desk for a small tin box, Sheriff Reyes paused before opening it. "Could be," he said hopefully. "Over a certain amount of time, that is. Lots of wanted men pass through these parts on their way to Old Mex. I just never had the resources to chase after them. A man could rake in a fair amount of reward money in a few short years."

From inside the cell, Oklahoma Bill said, "Go ahead and chase whoever you please. Won't take much for you to find a bullet with your name on it."

"The key stays with me whoever I chase, Bill," Reyes said. "You'd better hope I stay healthy long enough to unlock that damn door."

Still grumbling to Ed, who sat with his back against the cell's other wall, Bill sat on the edge of his cot and rested his arms over his knees.

"I couldn't stay on for any real amount of time," Slocum said.

"It's a nice town to settle in. No big problems apart from the occasional dust-up."

"Exactly. You're looking for a permanent resident and that ain't me. I'm more of a passerby."

"Then pass on by, asshole," Ed grumbled from the same cell.

Still wearing the easygoing smirk on his face, Slocum drew his pistol and pointed it at the prisoner. "And how much of a fuss do you think the sheriff will make if I move along after putting a hole through your ugly head?"

Ed didn't have an answer to that, and Reyes wasn't quick to squash the threat.

"That's what I thought." Slocum eased the Schofield back into its holster and shifted his attention back to the sheriff. "Appreciate the offer, Mark, but I think I'll take my money."

"Well, you wouldn't have to stay forever, John," Reyes said while opening the tin box and sifting through its contents. "Think it over and let me know if you'd like to spend some time here," he said while handing over his money. "However much you can give me, you won't regret it."

The moment the door was pulled open so Jack Halsey could shuffle inside, Slocum regretted staying in that office for as long as he had. Judging by the trouble Jack seemed to have in lifting his feet, one might have thought he was missing toes instead of fingers. He coddled his wounded arm against his chest, and on top of the layers of bandages the doctor had applied, there were now additional layers of old cloth as well as a thin jacket wrapped around that arm. Upon seeing Slocum in the office, Jack put on a weary smile and said, "There you are!"

"Yep," Slocum said. "Were you looking for me?"

Jack winced dramatically before saying, "Not at all. I just meant . . . there you are."

"And here I go." Tipping his hat to Reyes, Slocum said, "Good day to you, Sheriff. If you find yourself at the Dusty Hill, I'll gladly buy you a drink. Jack, hope that hand feels better, and as for you boys," he said while turning toward the cell, "well, you can rot in hell. Nice meeting you, gentlemen."

Apart from his tussle with Gwen under the sheets, walking out of the sheriff's office was the best Slocum had felt in a long while. The sun was bright in the sky, and the air was already warming around him. He had money in his pocket and a pretty lady waiting to help him spend it. Maybe nothing fancy as far as luxuries went, but they were more than welcome. Rather than walk straight back to the saloon, where he would very likely be drawn into a poker game that might last until the wee hours of the following morning, Slocum headed to the livery where his horse was being kept. One advantage to riding in the sheriff's posse was that his horse was given a stall free of charge. Oddly enough, that offer was made at the other livery in town that wasn't partly owned by Oscar, who wanted so desperately to be a lawman.

"Free ride ends now," the liveryman said. He was tall with skin that obviously wasn't accustomed to the desert sun. His features were distinctly Nordic, and his hair had the color and consistency of old straw. The coveralls hanging on his solid frame were just as faded as the sign nailed to the front of his stable.

Handing the man some money, Slocum asked, "How long will this cover me?"

"Through tonight."

"What? That should be good for at least three days!"

"I don't know where you got your information, mister," the liveryman said while holding Slocum's cash as if it were something he'd found beneath a moldy rock. "This here's only good for one day."

"Are you trying to make up for the money you lost when the sheriff told you to put up my horse as a courtesy for riding in the posse?"

The liveryman didn't say anything for or against that statement. He merely glanced up the street and said, "You want to use a badge to impress someone, go do business with Oscar. His place is right up that way."

"You know those men the sheriff and I brought in could very well have stolen every horse in here and set your barn on fire?"

The liveryman shrugged.

"Do you know I could set your barn on fire?"

"You want to rent a stall or not?"

"You've got my money," Slocum said. "I'll take the stall."

"You want greens along with the regular feed? It's extra."

Slocum thought of plenty he could say, but decided to pass up the chance. "That's all the money I'm handing out today, but I will be taking my horse for a ride. For some reason, I can't stand the smell around here."

"Suit yerself. I'll have the stall clean for you when you get back."

"Thank you kindly."

Slocum had ridden a light gray spotted stallion into town. The horse wasn't going to win any prizes, but it was hardy enough to brave the desert and had done just fine when tracking down Bill and his men. In fact, the stallion was so agreeable when he was saddled that Slocum felt badly for making him stare at such a jackass liveryman for most of the day.

"Mr. Slocum!" someone shouted.

When he led his horse outside and saw who was rushing across the street, Slocum practically jumped into his saddle.

"Wait! John!" Still cradling his arm, Jack Halsey picked up his pace as if he had every intention of throwing himself in front of Slocum's horse.

"Aw, hell," Slocum muttered to himself.

Jack was pale and covered in sweat. The wind that ripped through the middle of town cut Slocum to the bone, but acted like a splash of cold water on Jack's face. "Wonder if I could impose on you for a moment of time?"

"You can speak pretty well when you're not hollering like a lunatic," Slocum pointed out.

"Yeah, well, it ain't every day that I get my fingers chewed off. Maybe you would've handled it better?"

"I'd like to think so," Slocum replied, "but I see your point. What do you need?"

"I could use a ride to collect my horse and gear."

"So you do have a horse?" Slocum asked.

"Yes, sir. I was camping a few miles outside of town when I was attacked. Damn wolves caught me when I was out collecting firewood. Didn't see my horse right away and thought it might have been killed so I started running here before I lost the strength to do much else. Maybe my horse is dead, but maybe it ain't."

"You had plenty of strength when I saw you." Since he hadn't had another destination in mind apart from getting away from town for a little while, Slocum asked, "Where was your camp?"

"About three miles north of here. I can direct you when we get closer. If it's too much of an inconvenience, I understand."

"Nah, I was headed out anyways. The least I can do is take you back to your horse so you don't have to leave town the same way you came."

"Yeah," Jack chuckled. "Nobody wants that."

Slocum offered a hand to the other man, who reflexively started to take it with the one that was bundled up like a baby. Gritting his teeth, he curled that arm around so Slocum could take hold of his elbow and steady him while Jack climbed onto the stallion's back. It was a long, arduous process but he eventually settled into the saddle behind Slocum. They caught the attention of more than a few locals as they rode out of town.

6

Jack had picked a spot for his camp nestled between a cluster of low boulders that would have provided a nice wall against the cold night winds as he slept. It also would have lit up like the Fourth of July once a fire was started in the ring of rocks that had been built there. Once they were within ten yards of the boulders, Slocum reined his horse to a stop so Jack could climb down. He would have gotten a little closer, but the other man had become too fidgety to tolerate for one more second.

Hunching over to study the ground as he walked, Jack held his arm against his belly and paced a small tract of land. "Damn wolves didn't kill my horse. Not right here anyway."

Slocum looked down from where he sat and found the scuff marks on the rocky ground to mark the places where a shoed animal had walked. "Did you come from the west?"

"No."

"Then that's where your horse went. At least," Slocum said as he pointed to the tracks he'd found, "if that was your horse."

It took a few seconds for Jack to see the tracks that Slocum had spotted from his higher position, but found them nonetheless. "That's her all right!" he said excitedly as he took off running to follow the tracks down a slope. Jack moved with an awkward gait, probably because his feet were still sore from his frantic trek into town.

The slope led down to a crack in some rocks about sixty yards away from the camp. When he got a little closer, Slocum could tell the rocks were embedded in the ground and the crack was wider that he'd thought at first sight. "Hold up," he shouted. "Better steer clear of those rocks."

"I think my horse was here! The tracks lead to these rocks and it looks like she was runnin'!"

"That looks like a cave!" Slocum said. "Don't wolves live in caves?" Jack skidded to a stop, which gave Slocum a chance to draw the Winchester rifle from the boot of his saddle and lever in a round. "Back away," he said.

Jack was quick to comply and kept his eyes glued to the cave's entrance.

Slocum fired a shot into the shallow space. The bullet glanced off some rocks amid a shower of sparks and ricocheted within the darkness. Some dust trickled against the ground, but there wasn't another sound to be heard before he worked the rifle's lever again.

"I'm goin' in there," Jack said.

"You want to lose more than just a few fingers? Go right ahead."

"I won't lose nothin' because there ain't nothin' in there."

"Then why do you want to look inside? That cave's not big enough for a horse."

Jack took a few moments to try and sift through what Slocum thought was fairly simple logic. Even though he seemed to know what was being told to him, Jack waved him off and headed toward the cave anyway. "Something died in there," he said. "I can smell it. If one of them wolves crawled in here to perish after the fight I put up, I wanna know."

Slocum's instinct was to call the man back or drag him away from the cave. Since he had no connection to the lunatic other than having shared a doctor's office for a short stretch of time, he stayed put and readied the Winchester in case he got an easy shot at an angry wolf. If nothing else, there was always money to be made in selling pelts.

As if harkening back to his colorful entrance into Rocas Rojas, Jack hunched over and scrambled into the cave while hooting and hollering like a madman. His voice took an even higher pitch when he accidentally knocked his bundled right hand against a cave wall. He disappeared into the shadows, and before too long, his shouting subsided.

When Slocum thought he'd heard the heavy thump of a body hitting the ground, he shouted, "Jack? You all right?"

After a pause, a shaky reply came from the cave. "Yeah. I tripped. This cave goes back a little ways."

Owing to the angle of the sun and the fact that the ground was a uniform color around those rocks, Slocum wasn't able to pick out many details regarding the terrain. There was something strange about the echo coming from the cave, however. At first, Slocum thought his ears might be playing tricks on him. When he rode around the boulders to get a different vantage point, he found that the sound he'd heard had indeed come from two different spots. He climbed down from the saddle and approached the back end of the rock formation. "The cave opens up back here," he said.

"Yeah," Jack shouted from within the cave. "I can see some light."

The other side of the formation was a steep slope angling down from the rocks. The drop-off was only about six or seven feet, which was just enough to shade what was lying in the shallow pit. It was also enough to provide a barrier to keep the stench of dead meat from overwhelming him before. Now that he was looking straight down at the carcass, Slocum had to place a hand over his nose and mouth until he acclimated to the odors wafting up from there. "Think I found your horse," he said.

"What?"

Taking his hand away from his mouth, Slocum shouted, "I said I think I—"

Suddenly, Jack's head emerged from the back entrance of the cave. Because that opening was so much smaller than the one in front, it looked more like the rocks were passing him through their digestive tract and excreting him onto the desert floor. "I hear ya," he snarled. "No need to shout. Hey! That's my horse!"

"Looks like it may have slipped and broke its neck."

"Stay put! I'm comin' down there to get a look for myself!" Then, the rocks sucked his head back in as Jack began the arduous process of backing up and turning around within such cramped quarters.

Knowing that it would take a while for Jack to settle down long enough to escape, Slocum scrambled down the steep incline leading to the bottom of what had become a shallow, open grave. By the time he got within arm's reach of the horse's remains, Slocum had gotten as used to the scent as he was ever going to get. At least his stomach wasn't churning when he examined a few bloody spots along its side and neck.

Frantic scraping sounds followed by labored grunting announced Jack's reentry into the outside world. Those gave way to irregular footsteps as he circled around the rocks to where Slocum was conducting his examination. "Get away from there!" Jack snapped. "That's my horse!"

Without cowing to the other man's feverish demand, Slocum asked, "You said this animal was at your camp when you were attacked by wolves?"

"Yeah."

"Was that before or after it was shot?"

The anger that had been on Jack's face dropped away like a layer of dust blown off the rocks behind him. "Shot? What do you mean shot?"

"I mean the thing that happens when you point a gun at something and pull the trigger."

"Looks like she fell into that hole after getting chased by them damn wolves."

"This horse was shot and may have had enough left in her to run for a bit. What concerns me more is that you seem to have left something out of your story."

The anger returned to Jack's face as he approached Slocum. When he got close enough, another scent reached Slocum's nose that was almost as unpleasant as the dead horse.

"I don't owe you anything, Slocum," Jack said. "I asked for a favor and you were kind enough to help me out. That don't mean you're entitled to anything more than my gratitude."

"Maybe not, but I've been around long enough to know when to trust my instincts, and there's been something wrong with you from the moment you first staggered into town."

"Then leave me out here! I'll just take my . . ." When he looked down at his horse, Jack stared at the carcass and then turned accusing eyes back to the man that had brought him there. "Were you sifting through my bags?"

Slocum scowled at Jack and then turned to look into the pit. He'd barely noticed the saddlebags since he'd been too distracted by the gunshot wounds. "Why would I go through your bags?"

"Someone's been through them. They're all crooked and open!"

"Well, the damn horse is just laying there!" Slocum said. "Anyone could've gone through those bags. Hell, those wolves could've poked their noses through them for all I know!"

Jack's right hand moved toward his holster, but stopped short. Until that moment, Slocum had all but forgotten about

the pieced-together firearm he'd taken away from him at the
doctor's office. The gun must have been returned to Jack
along with his other belongings when he'd left Bower's
care.

"Them bags are mine," Jack said as he crossed his left
hand over his belly toward the holster. "Along with everything that's in 'em."

Slocum stepped back. "You're right. Those are your possessions. But you're not right about me poking through
them. All I did was take a look at the horse because those
gunshot wounds don't match up to what you said before.
You don't owe me any explanations. Guess this whole thing
just seems peculiar."

When Jack smiled, it wasn't a pretty sight. Yellowed teeth
were bared, as well as several gaps where teeth had once
been. Even without the irregularly spaced holes, the gri-
mace still would have been unsettling. "I'm the one that
lost some fingers to a damn wolf and you want to talk about
peculiar?"

"What's that on your hand?" Slocum asked.

Jack shifted his attention to his left hand, which was
smeared with a thick, dark substance running up past his
wrist. "Must've stuck it in something when I was crawlin'
through that cave."

"Looks like dung. Smells like it, too."

"Well, there were wolves in there! They ain't the clean-
est animals, you know!"

"What did you do? Try to smear it on the walls? It's all
over you!"

"Aw, leave me be," Jack said while making his way to
the bottom of the pit. Hunkering down over the dead animal
to stick his hand into the saddlebag, he took out a dented
canteen and some jerked beef, which he smelled before
pitching it toward the dead horse's rump. Curling his bundled hand against his chest, Jack dug all the way down to

the bottom of the bag as if he were sticking his arm straight down the horse's throat. "It ain't here."

"What isn't there?"

"Oh, wait. It should be in the other bag. Wanna give me a hand with this?"

"Well, since you asked so nicely," Slocum replied as he crossed his arms and made it perfectly clear he had no intention of getting any closer to that carcass.

"Look, even with both hands I couldn't roll this thing over. Can you help me or not?"

"What's so important?"

"It's something that someone was after when they went through my bags. Without it, all I got is half a hand and the clothes on my back."

Many times, Slocum wished he didn't have a conscience. As far as he could tell, the damn things only got a man into trouble.

"So," Jack said, "you gonna help me or did you come all this way to laugh at a cripple while he tries to scrape up whatever's left of his earthly possessions?"

"You're not a cripple."

Jack muttered a few other things before placing a foot on the horse's ribs to give him some leverage as he grabbed hold of the saddlebag and started to pull. His first attempt didn't do much of anything, so he looped his right arm beneath the leather bag for a more secure grip as he leaned back and pulled with every bit of strength his body could muster. The bag didn't even budge before Jack lost his grip along with his balance and fell straight back to bounce off the edge of the pit. When he flopped over and propped himself up, the hand smeared with dung slid on the rocks and his chest bounced off the desert floor.

"All right," Slocum said as he walked over to where Jack had fallen and grabbed his elbow. "On your feet."

"Bless you," Jack sighed.

"I don't know about blessings, but I sure won't be earning anything of the sort if I stood by to watch any more of this."

"Whatever compels you . . . I'll take it." Once he was on his feet, Jack dusted himself off and looked down at the horse. "Any ideas of how we could get to those bags?"

"Actually, yes."

Slocum's first idea was to rig some sort of lever using a piece of wood or a fallen log. Since neither of those things or even a viable substitute could be seen, he decided on another route. He tied one end of a length of rope to his saddle horn and the other end to the horn of the saddle still buckled to the dead horse. With a bit of encouragement and some elbow grease applied at the right time, Slocum and Jack were able to pull the saddlebags free.

"I hope your valuables weren't breakable," Slocum said while untying the rope from each saddle. "Because that bag's flat as a pancake."

"All I'm worried about is one thing," Jack said while anxiously sticking his hand into the scuffed bag. He grinned when he added, "Better make that a couple hundred things." The prize in his hand was wrapped in what looked to be an old scarf. Part of the dirty cloth fell away to reveal a bundle of cash large enough to back his claim.

"Good thing those wolves weren't too greedy," Slocum said.

"Right. About them wolves." Jack pulled out wads of cash and stuffed the money into whatever pockets he could reach. The bills that remained were jammed down one of his boots. "I want you to help me track 'em down."

"Why?"

"Because now I can pay you is why."

"No," Slocum said. "I meant why would you want to track down those wolves? You found your camp. You got your money. I can take you back to town and you can buy a new horse. From then on, you must have better things to do than chase a bunch of animals."

"You know anything about Injun beliefs?"

"No, and I doubt a man who calls them Injuns knows much either."

"I can call 'em whatever I want on account of I was raised by one until I ran away from home to strike out on my own. I know what I was taught and I got plenty worse names for the son of a bitch that taught 'em to me."

Slocum had heard people come up with much worse names for their family than that, so he nodded and said, "Go on."

"Before my adopted uncle died, a doctor hacked off his leg and buried it in a field. I was told he wouldn't be able to thrive in the afterlife until he was whole again."

"What tribe was your uncle from?"

"That don't matter," Jack replied. "What matters is that the family wasn't the same because we weren't able to find that damn field. I was forced to dig up half that county, but we didn't find a single bone."

"You sure about that? I've met members of several different tribes and never—"

"Maybe my uncle and everyone else in my family was touched in the head."

Slocum didn't have any trouble believing that one.

"But what I know for sure," Jack continued, "is that anyone who ever knew my uncle had a string of bad luck that lasted for years after we let him rot without his leg. Whether it's Injun curses or a crock o' shit, I know what I saw and I don't want my luck to get any worse than it already is."

"But you gotta know that your fingers are gone. There isn't anything left but . . . well . . . they're just gone."

"I know that." Jack stuck his right hand out as he said, "I also know that I won't be able to rest until I find the animals that did this to me!"

"You want vengeance on a wolf?"

"I want to find it and skin the son of a bitch. At the very least, I'll be able to say that anything that does this to Jack Halsey gets a whole lot more than a good meal."

If Slocum had had any doubt that Jack was cracked, he didn't have it anymore. There was ferocity in his eyes that no man could fake, no matter how great an actor or bluffer he may have been. He'd also seen a few cases where a man who got mauled by a bear or gored by a bull couldn't rest until he'd proved he was better than the animal by making it pay for the damage it had done to him. It wasn't exactly rational, but that wasn't much of a concern when a man's blood ran that hot. Any living thing, man or beast, tended to lash out when it was wounded.

Perhaps sensing Slocum's slow change of spirit, Jack said, "And then there's the matter of the well-being of folks in that town."

"How so?"

"That wolf got a taste o' human flesh and blood! It's a man-eater! Once that happens, there ain't no turnin' back."

"That doesn't mean it'll lead a rampage on Rocas Rojas."

"It don't bode well for anyone else that happens to stumble upon that pack. Would you have it on your conscience when some bunch of kids or a lady gets ripped apart by those beasts?"

Slocum shook his head. "This is sounding dumber the more I think about it. Have you ever tried to track wolves? It's no picnic on regular terrain, but this is rock and sand!"

"It's possible, though."

"You want to find those wolves so badly?" Slocum asked. "Wait here for them to come back to this cave. They'll probably revisit a den especially if there's fresh meat laying here."

"They already moved on."

Slocum studied the other man carefully. Once he got a

good feel for Jack's face, he watched for the slightest change when he asked, "This isn't about the wolves, is it?"

"What do you mean?"

"Your horse was shot. Did you shoot it?"

"Why would I shoot my own goddamn horse miles away from town?"

"Then that means there were armed men here to do the shooting. Could it be you're after them?"

"No," Jack sighed, "I was lucky enough to scare those wolves away once I got to my gun. After that, I don't know what the hell happened. I barely know how I got to that doctor's office. I still wanna go after them wolves."

"On account of your Indian background?"

"That's right."

Slocum sighed, not believing everything Jack said, but looking at enough evidence to back up some of it. As for the rest, there was always a good dose of craziness to explain it. All Slocum needed to do was look into Jack's eyes to find that much.

"Can you at least take me back to town?" Jack asked.

"As long as it's right now. I've smelled enough of this horse to last me for a while."

"Amen to that."

7

The ride back to town was quiet and uneventful. If not for the fact that he had a smelly, off-kilter vagrant clinging to him, Slocum might have gone so far as to call it peaceful. Having the stink of dead flesh lodged in his nose didn't help matters, but Slocum did his best to enjoy the scenery and fresher air as he rode the trail that took him into Rocas Rojas.

Once they were in town, he rode directly to Oscar's horse trading and rental business. After an arduous bargaining process with the stuffed shirt who fancied himself a lawman, Jack purchased a gelding that had some spirit and most of its teeth. Its coloring made Slocum uncertain as to whether the horse's coat was just black or if it was so dirty that a dozen baths could no longer do any good. Jack was liberal with the money he'd taken from the saddlebags, which was allowed him to get a blanket along with a new set of reins. Oscar tried to gouge him on the price of the saddle, but Slocum had enough pull with the local man to avoid that trap.

"I saw that thing before," Slocum said while tapping the battered hunk of leather.

"Sure," Oscar replied. "You've seen what I got for sale."

"No, this wasn't with the other saddles." After thinking it over long enough for the other man to stew, Slocum snapped his fingers and said, "Now I remember! This is what you were using to hold the back door of your barn open while you were shoveling out the stalls!"

Jack fixed a glare onto Oscar and made an offer that was just over half the one he'd been considering before hearing that bit of news.

Reluctantly, Oscar agreed. "Give me the money and get the hell out of my sight."

"That's no way to speak to your customers," Jack said while counting out the money. "We might get upset and come back to teach you some manners."

At first, Oscar didn't seem impressed. Then, the hand he held out for the money began to shake and his eyes widened. "Sorry about that. I'm just trying to earn a living."

"I understand."

"You and your friends are welcome back anytime."

"That's good to hear." Jack blinked and then asked, "Did you say friends? You mean someone other than him?"

"No," Slocum said. "Not me. I think he means them."

Jack was the only one not looking at Main Street, and when he did shift his gaze in that direction, he immediately dropped the saddle he was holding. "Shit!"

"You know them?" Slocum asked.

"Yeah. Where's the damn horse?"

Oscar was rooted to his spot. As soon as Jack had dropped his things and bolted into the stable, the four men riding down the street drew their pistols and charged.

Slocum drew his Schofield and dove at Oscar to push him out of harm's way. Both of them hit the ground hard as the first wave of gunshots tore through the air above them. Firing toward the riders as he got back to his feet, Slocum asked, "Who the hell are they?"

"Robbers!" Jack shouted from directly behind him.

Having found the horse he'd just bought, he'd regained enough of his senses to realize he needed his saddle and reins to best ride away from there.

"Are they the ones who shot your horse?"

Another burst of gunfire ripped through the air and tore into the stable's wide front door. "Looks that way."

"What are they after?"

"My money! They must've known I had it and they probably thought I wouldn't have just left it. Must've followed my tracks back here."

Oscar had gotten to his feet as well. Although he'd found an old hunting rifle, he didn't seem ready to use it. "Get these men away from my livestock before any of them gets shot!"

"Working on it," Slocum said as he sighted along the top of his pistol. From the instant he pulled the trigger, he knew it would be a miss. However, the round blazed close enough to the group of men to scatter them in two directions. Some of them rounded a corner that would allow them to circle around the stable, and the rest peeled away to charge down a wide alley between two neighboring buildings.

Slocum took the opportunity to replace the spent rounds from his pistol with fresh ones from his gun belt. Now that the riders were no longer shooting at him, Oscar fired several shots in their general direction.

"Get that horse saddled and ride out the back," Slocum said.

"But they'll just come after me," Jack replied.

"That's the idea. If they're after you, then we should be able to lead them away from here."

Oscar couldn't nod fast enough when he said, "I like that idea."

"Shut up and get that back door open," Slocum said while collecting his horse. He could have been in his saddle and galloping away if not for the fact that Jack was still struggling with the buckles of the rig he'd just bought.

Once again, a pang from that damn conscience of his put Slocum into the line of fire.

"How long have these men been after you?" Slocum asked while cinching one of the other man's buckles tight enough to hold the saddle in place.

"They must've seen the money I took from those saddlebags. They probably shot my horse, too."

The sound of approaching horses came from two directions as both groups of riders converged on the stable. Oscar ran back and forth between the back door and a window that looked out to where hay bales were stacked. "Will you two just get the hell away from here!"

"That money's all I've got!" Jack said. "I sold my house back in Arizona."

"You're so full of shit," Slocum growled. "Those men are chasing after you."

"I see them!" Oscar squealed.

"What difference does it make where they came from or who the hell they are?" Jack asked. "They're firing at us here and now!"

"The difference is between me getting mixed up with them or letting you fellows work things out amongst yourselves."

"The other ones are circling around," Oscar said. "Clear off my property! All of you!"

Outside, the hooves came to a rest and one man spoke up. "Send the little pecker with the seven fingers outside or we're burning that whole place down."

That one nearly caused Oscar to soil himself.

"We came for Jack Halsey!" the man outside said. "Send him out or we'll drag him out."

Jack climbed into his saddle and reached across his belly to draw his pistol. "Looks like we found our horse killers. We can still draw them away, but you gotta agree to help me find them wolves once we put these assholes to rest."

Farther down the street, people shouted and a woman

screamed. One familiar voice rose above the rest when it shouted, "You men clear out of here or we'll open fire."

"God damn it," Slocum snarled. "That's Stan. Where's the sheriff?"

"I don't know," Oscar told him. "Why don't you leave my property and find out?"

Slocum pulled himself onto his horse and flicked the reins. He hadn't been in Rocas Rojas for long, but he did know that the would-be deputies were more apt to get themselves shot than hit anything in front of them. Beyond that, the commotion outside told him that locals were gathering to get a look at what was happening near the stable. That meant they were in the line of fire. "Why are they after you, Jack?"

"They knew about the money I was carrying as well as some other valuables. Like I said before, I sold my house and I'm carrying everything that's worth a dime. They were closing in on me before and were chased away by them wolves. They probably figured I was dead, came back to rummage through my saddlebags, and then followed us back here."

"You're still full of shit!" Slocum growled. "Why didn't you tell me this before?"

"Because I thought you wouldn't want any part of helping me. If you keep the job I offered, I'll double your fee."

"We ain't even discussed a real fee, but when we do, it'll be a big one."

"Agreed!"

"Fine," Slocum said. "We'll lead them to those trees just south of town. You know the ones I mean?"

Jack nodded. "I think so."

"They're just past the town limits. When you see them, charge straight down the path. Just keep going and don't follow me. Shoot as many of them as you can."

"I may not be much use with a gun in my left hand."

"Just keep shooting," Slocum said. "Leave the rest to me."

They exploded from the stable amid a chorus of hollers

and thundering hooves. Slocum and Jack had their pistols ready, but refrained from firing just yet. The intention was to make noise, not waste valuable ammunition. The first group of riders who'd split off were approaching the stable from the left and immediately charged after them. Slocum could hear a rifle shot along with Oscar's voice as more hooves rumbled through the stable itself. After a few seconds, the other group of riders followed in Slocum's wake and emerged from the back end of the stable after charging through from the front.

Slocum and Jack rode south toward the town's limits. Fortunately, they could see the edge of town from just about anywhere inside it, and the cluster of trees stood like a beacon along the right side of the trail. Both of them reached the trees as hot lead began hissing around them. As Jack continued down the trail, Slocum pulled back on his reins. By the time he had enough trees around him to provide a scant amount of cover, his horse was churning to a stop and Jack was pounding straight ahead.

The first two riders were hot on their heels. One of them might have seen Slocum dismount because he slowed down. His partner charged through the patch of woods, just in time for Slocum to catch him with a well-placed shot. His bullet hit the rider high in the body, and the impact sent him spiraling from his saddle. Even though the first rider seemed to be more aware of what was waiting inside those trees, he still wasn't quick enough to avoid it. He pulled back hard on his reins, causing his horse to rear up and churn its front legs in the air. Slocum waited for the horse to drop down before firing again. Neither of the two shots hit, but they succeeded in convincing the rider to point his horse in another direction as the remaining men thundered up behind him.

As the horsemen gathered to formulate a plan, they were blindsided by a flurry of gunshots. Judging by the sick coughing sound of the gun and the fact that none of the men were hit, Slocum knew they'd come from Jack. He joined in with a few shots of his own to make the pair of guns sound like a real ambush. Just as the riders began to rally for a charge into the trees, one of them was hit and fell in spectacular fashion. His head snapped back, his upper body twisted around, and blood sprayed through the air as he toppled from his saddle. To make an even bigger spectacle, one of his feet was caught in its stirrup so he hung from his horse like a rag doll.

After that, two of the riders broke away and one held his ground. The one that stayed had a thick mane of black-and-gray hair emerging from beneath a wide-brimmed hat. He spotted Slocum and was sighting in on him when the horse with the wounded man hanging from its saddle bucked in front of him to inadvertently block the shot.

Slocum holstered the Schofield and drew the Winchester from its boot. As soon as the rifle's stock touched his shoulder, he began firing in a steady torrent, slowed only by the need to lever in fresh rounds. The riders in his sights would have headed for town, but were met by another crackling series of gunshots. Those came from Sheriff Reyes's gun as the lawman rode down the trail from Rocas Rojas. With only one option that didn't involve riding into incoming fire, the attackers steered away from the path and raced into the surrounding desert.

Reyes kept riding and firing at the retreating men. The surviving gunmen pulled outside of pistol range and didn't show any signs of slowing down. Slocum kept his rifle at the ready, but the man who was left behind was in no condition to pose a threat. The only thing he was suited for was filling a hole marked by a simple wooden cross.

The lawman returned and reloaded his weapon. "What was that about?" he asked.

"They came to try and rob us," Slocum explained. "Must have seen the money my friend here was carrying. You might want to get back and make sure they don't double back and try to stir up any more trouble."

The sheriff's jurisdiction was so small that all he needed to do was glance back at the little town to see the street in front of his office was clear. "Looks fine for now," he said, "but I'll head on back. Sure I can't convince you to stay on and keep watch over the prisoner until Judge Morrow comes along to hold a trial?"

"I've got some work to do away from here," Slocum said. "Better pay. Also, taking this one far away from here would be the best favor I could do for Rocas Rojas."

Reyes nodded and cast a disparaging look at Jack, who was making his way back to them. To Slocum, he said, "The offer for a job is still open if you like."

"Thanks but no thanks," Slocum said. "The money I got for Bill was more than enough for now."

"Suit yourself. You'd make a hell of a good deputy and that offer won't be goin' anywhere."

"Much obliged, Sheriff. I need to collect my things from the saloon and then I'll be moving on."

Reyes tipped his hat to Slocum, made a lesser gesture to Jack, and then rode back into town. Once the lawman was gone, Slocum said, "You've got the time it takes for me to get back to the Dusty Hill to convince me why I shouldn't feed you to the next bunch of wolves I find."

Flicking his reins to fall into step beside him, Jack spoke in a rush of words that spilled out like water through a leaky bucket. "From what I saw of them tracks at the cave, those wolves were headed in about the same direction as those men."

"What are the odds?" Slocum grumbled.

Either ignoring or missing the sarcasm in his voice, Jack said, "Exactly! When Fate reaches out to shake yer hand, you'd be a damn fool to slap it away."

"Uh-huh."

"I need protection while going after those wolves, and you wanna make some money without being tied down to any piss hole of a town like this."

That was a bit extreme, but Slocum could relate to the sentiment. "Go on."

"You think I'm crazy? Fine. You've seen my money, so you know I can pay you to ride along and humor me as I take back what's mine."

Slocum had played more than enough poker to know when another man had accidentally given away a bit of information he'd been trying to guard. "You're not crazy enough to think you'll get your fingers back."

"No," Jack sighed. "But I do want to reclaim something that one of them wolves swallowed. It's a ring."

"A ring?"

"Yes. What's so hard to believe about that?"

Despite taking a much slower pace going into town as they'd had when leaving it, the two men were still about to cross back into Rocas Rojas when Slocum asked, "What about all of that Indian ancestry talk?"

"That's not quite the whole truth."

"And why hide it from me until now?"

"Because the ring has more than sentimental value to me. It's the most valuable thing I took from my old house, and when I sell it, I should have enough to buy a nice little piece of land and maybe even start a little farm."

Slocum looked over to the scruffy man and had to laugh. "Now you want to be a farmer?"

"I don't know. I just want my ring back so I can sell it. If I would'a told you about it before, maybe you would have tracked down that wolf to get it yourself. It would certainly be worth the effort. Now I know you ain't the sort of man who'd do such a thing."

"At this point, I don't even know if I can believe a damn word that comes out of your mouth. I've lost track of how much bullshit you've told me already. Is your name even Jack Halsey?"

Sitting up in his saddle and puffing out his chest, he replied, "It most certainly is! And here," he added while digging into his pocket to pull out a small wad of cash. "As a token of goodwill, I'll pay part of your fee in advance."

Slocum reined his horse to a stop and looked at the money in Jack's hand. It wasn't enough to retire on, but was more than enough to procure his services as a tracker or guide. "That's only part of the fee?"

"Remember what I said about those men being after me?"

"Yeah."

"That part wasn't bullshit. If you doubt that—"

Slocum stopped him with a raised hand. "I don't doubt it. After the short amount of time I've known you, I already could see why someone would go through the trouble of hunting you down to put a bullet through your skull."

Although Jack was relieved to be taken at face value, he wasn't so grateful once the rest of Slocum's words sank in.

"I'm guessing you want more than just help in tracking down some wolves," Slocum continued.

"That's right. Normally I can take care my myself, but I shoot with my right hand. Seeing as you're held in such high regard by a lawman, I'm thinking I can trust you to do the job I'm paying you for without getting greedy."

"But there will be more of that fee coming than what you're holding now?"

"That's why I said it's only part of it."

"All right," Slocum said as he took the money from Jack's hand. "I don't care about any Indian burial legends, tales about your family, sob stories about your jewelry, or promises about getting on Fate's good side for taking back what was stolen from you. You want to hire a scout who can watch your back along the way? Fine."

"We got to be quick about it," Jack said. "I figure it'll only be another day or so before what's lodged in that wolf's belly will find its way out."

"Hold on," Slocum said. "Is that why you had dung all over your hands back at that cave? You were sifting through wolf scat?"

"It was worth a shot."

"If there's any more of that to be done, you're the one to do it."

"Agreed," Jack said as he extended his hand to be shaken. Slocum passed on the offer.

8

The trading post was ten miles southeast of Rocas Rojas. Tacked on to a stagecoach stopover point, it wasn't in sight of anything other than rocks, sand, and the occasional jackrabbit. Even stagecoaches had become a rare sight, but that didn't mean the place didn't get its visitors. An old man and his wife ran the trading post and posted the schedule for coaches that would roll past on their way to better places. The old man kept a shotgun nearby and did his best to make a sale to the men who appreciated such a perfect, out-of-the-way location to conduct illicit business.

A horse thundered up to the trading post and circled the place. After reaching the front door again, its rider waved toward the north to signal the other two that had been following him. The first man climbed down from his saddle, removing his hat and bandanna to reveal a long face framed by black hair intermixed with silvery gray strands. His brushy mustache had the same salt-and-pepper coloring, and his eyes narrowed menacingly as he approached the old man behind the counter.

"You'd be looking for the Italian fella?" the old man asked.

The new arrival nodded.

Hooking a thumb toward a door in the back of the trading post, the old man said, "Him and the other one's back there. Make it quick and get out."

The old man's wife peeked out through a window opening into a small kitchen, where hot meals were prepared for passengers waiting for the next stagecoach to arrive.

"Too late for breakfast?" the man with the black-and-silver hair asked.

"No, sir. Whatever you like."

"Eggs and bacon. Toast with marmalade if you got it."

"We do."

"Have it ready soon. I don't intend on staying long."

The old fellow's face brightened somewhat when he heard that, but became worried again when the other two men stepped in from outside.

"Still ain't no one behind us, Dan," one of the two men said.

Scowling in a way that curled his brushy, graying mustache, Dan said, "Keep watch and let me know the moment you see anyone coming this way. I don't care how many or who it is. You let me know as soon as you see anything bigger than a coyote approach this place."

"Don't we even get a taste of water?"

Reluctantly, Dan nodded and looked at the old man. "Don't give them one drop of liquor, you hear me?"

"Yes, sir, I do."

Confident that his warnings would be heeded, Dan pushed open the door to the back room and stepped inside. It was a cramped space that was just large enough to hold two chairs and a small desk littered with what looked to be the old man's accounting ledgers and a few out-of-date newspapers. Sitting behind that desk as if he owned it as well as the rest of the trading post was a balding gentleman with dark, olive-colored skin. He stood up and extended a hand across the desk while saying, "I heard you were riding with Bill Dressel these days, Mr. Walsh."

"You look surprised to see me."

"I am, especially since Oklahoma Bill was chased out of Texas and presumed dead."

Dan shook the Italian man's hand and glanced over to the wall beside the door. A short gunman with a nasty scar running along the side of his face stood like a shadow in the corner. "Bill's not dead. Who's the ghost?"

"That's Zack. Do you know who I am?"

"You're filler for a shallow grave unless you tell that ghost of yours to stand so's I can see him plainly."

The man in the corner didn't move. Even after getting a nod from the Italian, Zack took a minimum number of steps toward the desk.

"I'm Salvatore Majesco," the Italian said. "You're Dan Walsh, but the only other associate of yours that I'm aware of was Mr. Dressel and one of his partners by the name of Edward Meeks."

"Both of them are in jail and the rest of Bill's men are dead as far as I know."

"That's unfortunate."

"Only for Bill, Ed, and those dead men."

Salvatore stood and hooked his thumbs into his vest pockets. Although his black wool pants bore the dust from a ride into the trading post, there wasn't enough of it to have come from making the ride on horseback. More than likely, he'd been waiting for a stagecoach as well as Dan Walsh. "I take it you weren't very close to Bill."

"I went into the town where he was tossed into jail," Dan said. "Got one of my boys killed along the way. I owe Bill that much and no more. If he's stupid enough to get himself caught and locked up that tight, he's on his own."

Dan reached into his pocket for a cigarette and lit it with a match he struck against the side of the desk. "Maybe he'll learn his lesson the hard way."

"Or maybe he'll get hung."

The cigarette burned as Dan drew in a stream of smoke. Exhaling it through his nostrils, he wheezed, "Problem solved either way. What the hell do you care which it is?"

"All I care about is getting my money back. I can't do that very well if the men I hired for the job are too busy trading shots with lawmen."

"Made my run at that town and am through with it. Bill ain't here to meet with you, but I am. You wanna tell me about the job or do you care enough to get Bill out yerself?"

Salvatore considered that for a moment and then shrugged. "You're the second in command Bill told me about?"

"That's right. We parted ways back in Oklahoma. I took the quiet way out of a dispute with a bunch of federal marshals while he shot up enough of them to earn a nickname attached to that piece of flat land. We kept in touch, but I only take the well-paying jobs. Bill's got a taste for any bit of excitement he can scrape up. That's why he took to robbing stagecoaches and general stores when he should've been laying low. I got word that an Italian fella had his sights set on a man named Jack Halsey and was willing to pay enough to warrant my attention. Bill sent word to me letting me know the general whereabouts of this Halsey fella so here I am. That," Dan said while pulling in another lungful of smoke, "is the last bit of explanation you'll get from me. Do you still have a job you need done or not?"

"I do, sir. Jack Halsey took something that belongs to me."

"He skinned out of Rocas Rojas. Any notion where he'd be heading from there?"

"He's not exactly a man with roots. The last time I saw him was in West Texas. That's where I met up with your former associate. It seems quite fortunate that he's still in the New Mexico Territory instead of deciding to ride in another direction altogether."

"Not as such," Dan said. "Texas Rangers have been looking for a gang that robbed a few banks in Dallas and San Antonio. Anyone looking to get across the border into Mexico will have an easier time heading through these parts and going south. Only danger is if the man you're after decides to hop a northbound train and take his chances with getting to Canada."

"He won't," Salvatore said with supreme confidence. "He needs to get closer to the Mexico border sooner or later. That much I know for certain."

Dan savored his cigarette for the better portion of a minute before speaking up again. "What did Jack Halsey take from you?"

"That's not your concern."

"It is if my fee depends on recovering this stolen property," Dan replied. "What if he hides this property away for safekeeping? He could hand me a pocket watch and I wouldn't know if I got what I needed or not."

"All you need to do is bring him to me along with whatever is on his person at the time."

"So you want him alive, huh?"

"Most definitely," Salvatore said.

"That's gonna cost extra."

"I offered Bill five thousand dollars to be split among him and his men however he saw fit. I can offer you the same amount. If you get the job done yourself or if you bring along a thousand men at five dollars apiece, I don't care. Just bring me Jack Halsey and anything he might have had on his person."

Clamping his teeth around what was left of his cigarette, Dan extended a hand to Salvatore. "You got yourself a deal. Will you be setting up shop here until I bring your man back?"

"No," the Italian said as he shook Dan's hand. "When there's news or if you need to contact me for any other reason, contact me by telegraph. Here's all the information you need."

Even though Dan had been trying to keep an eye on Zack, the man with the scarred face still crept up on him like a ghost. Every one of Dan's muscles tensed, but the only gesture Zack made was to stretch out a hand that had a business card wedged between two fingers. As promised, the card contained contact information that would allow a telegram to be sent to the Italian from any office with wire service. Pocketing the card, Dan blew smoke into Zack's face just to see if he could get a reaction from the stoic gunman.

He couldn't.

"This is my job now," Dan said. "If Bill gets out of his cage and comes sniffing around . . ."

Salvatore shook his head while pulling on his jacket. "Unless he does so in the next two hours, he won't find me. I've already missed one coach while waiting for you gentlemen and I don't intend on missing another. The only other way for Mr. Dressel to contact me is if you share the information on that card with him. As I said already, if you want a partner in this endeavor, that's up to you. The fee remains the same."

"Well then, I'd best be off." Dan stepped out of the small office, but made sure not to turn his back to Salvatore's ghost. When it became necessary to walk through the front door of the trading post, he swore he could feel Zack's eyes boring through the back of his skull. The old woman emerged from the kitchen with his food already wrapped up and seemed grateful that he wasn't about to stop and eat it there.

The two men that had accompanied Dan to the trading post were outside with the horses. Karl was a squat fellow who looked as if his torso had been crudely whittled from a tree stump. His head was just a bit too big for his body, which made it seem as if he was always about to topple over when he walked. The second man's name was Young. Dan guessed that was his last name, but had never bothered asking for confirmation. Compared to Karl, Young was skinny. Of course, everyone was skinny when they stood next to Karl.

"You find the Italian?" Young asked.

"Sure did. Remember what Bill told us when we parted ways in Texas?"

"Yeah."

"Seems that little bastard he was chasing really was carrying something that was valuable."

"It's with that horse!" Karl said. "I told you we didn't do a good enough job in searching them saddlebags!"

"It ain't with the horse. Them two already went back and searched that carcass. Whatever Jack was carrying that was so valuable, he wouldn't just leave it behind. He's got it or he knows where it is, but he wouldn't leave it with that dead animal. We need to ride back to that town where Bill's being kept."

"Why? You think we can bust him out?"

"No. Actually, you should go. I don't think anyone got a real good look at you."

Young's ratlike face twisted in disapproval and didn't find any comfort by glancing over to Karl. Finally, he asked, "What am I gonna do?"

Rather than ask the other two to follow him away from the trading post, Dan mounted his horse and simply started riding. The others fell into step quickly enough and the three of them were putting the little structure behind them before Salvatore or his gunman stepped outside.

"We're taking up the job that Bill was too incompetent to do," Dan said after they were far enough away from the trading post to have some privacy.

"Incompetent?" Karl sputtered. "He wouldn't take too kindly to bein' called that."

Dan was quick to reply, "I'm sure he wouldn't, but he won't hear me say that. You know why? He's in a jail cell. You know why he's there? He's incompetent."

"Guess you got a point there." Despite his agreement, Karl's voice was so low that he seemed nervous about being overheard.

"We're after a man named Jack Halsey. Bill was tracking him through West Texas when he got rounded up by that posse on his way here."

"Was he one of them fellas we chased out of that stable?" Young asked.

"I think so. Bill was the only one that got a good look at him. He had a picture that he showed me, but I want to make sure that's Halsey before we chase the wrong man across every territory under the sun. I also wanna know about the other man that was with him. Halsey was alone all this time and now he's got someone doin' his shootin' for him. That asshole already killed Jeremiah and I want to know if he's a lawman or just some hired hand. You go into town, ask at the hotel or saloon or back at that livery about those men."

"I been scouting before," Young said. "I know how to look for someone."

"Fine. Then do it. Don't wear your gun. Change your clothes. Make sure you don't look the same as when we were there before."

"Try taking a bath," Karl offered.

Before Young could get his nose bent too far out of joint, Dan said, "That should make a difference. At least splash some water on your face to wash off a few layers of grime."

"Got anything else to say?" Young asked.

"Yeah," Dan replied. "If you mess this up and get caught, you're on yer own."

9

Slocum began his search back at the cave. Now that he had more of a purpose for being there, he dismounted and tied his horse to a tree so he could take a closer look for himself. He'd done a fair amount of tracking, but could think of other men who were better suited for the job. Time was a factor, and there was always a chance that Jack might come to his senses to realize what a fool's errand they were on before paying the agreed-upon fee, so Slocum put his nose to the grindstone and got to work.

"Why are we still here?" Jack whined.

"Isn't this the last place you saw those wolves that attacked you?" Slocum asked.

"Yes."

"Then these tracks are the ones we want to follow. Can't exactly expect much success if we start off following the wrong trail. Maybe you should help me instead of complaining."

Jack lent his eyes to the task of picking up the trail left by the wolves, but didn't stop muttering under his breath while cradling his wounded hand. Although Slocum knew the wounds were bad, he was amused by the fact that the pain became worse when it was time to do something other than talk.

"I think they headed east," Slocum said.

"You sure about that?"

He wasn't, but admitting as much wasn't going to make life any easier. "As sure as I can be."

"That don't sound good."

"If you know so much about tracking wolves, then let me know. Are you even certain they were wolves?"

Holding out his bandaged hand, Jack wailed, "I saw 'em close enough, didn't I?"

"Maybe they were coyotes."

"What difference does it make?"

Slocum squatted down to a large patch of mud surrounding a portion of rock that was shaped like a giant dent in the ground. The sides were angled only slightly, but were steep enough to have collected some of the water that fell during a short bout of rain that had passed through a few nights ago. Most of it had dried off and the rest was lapped up by the horses. In fact, Slocum's horse had been the one to make the find. Pointing down to the hardened mud surrounding the puddle, Slocum asked, "Those look like coyote or wolf prints to you?"

Jack rushed over so quickly that Slocum almost had to stop him from trampling over the prints he'd discovered. He skidded to a halt a few paces shy of doing any damage and placed his hands upon his knees while hunkering down for a closer look. At least he tried to place his hands on his knees. The moment his bandaged right hand touched his leg, he let out a pained yelp and shifted into a wobbly sideways stance. "There's a whole bunch of tracks," he said. "I think some might be deer or elk or something like that. Are there elk around here?"

"You're not much of a hunter, are you?" Pointing down

to a section of mud directly across from where his horse was drinking, Slocum said, "Those right there. That's what I'm talking about."

"Yeah. Those do look like wolf tracks. Some sorta big dog anyways."

"I'd say about the size of a small wolf or a large coyote. The storm that came through was about the right time for when your wolf pack would have still been here. Did they get to you before or after the rain fell?"

Jack closed his eyes and thought about it for a few seconds. "That night's kind of a mess when I try to think about it."

"Looks like plenty of animals came along to drink from here, but these are some of the freshest tracks in this mud. If the rain came before you were attacked, they may have been put down when the pack passed here before meeting up with you. Or it could have been some other pack. It's not like there's a shortage of coyotes around here."

"No," Jack said sharply. "These are the same hellhounds that got to me. I know it."

"Hellhounds?" Slocum chuckled. "I thought them being wolves was pushing it."

"Laugh all you want. I know these are the tracks we're after because it was raining when I started walking into town to get to that doctor. Makes sense for them to have gone into the cave for shelter that night because it was pouring! Then they came by here to drink before heading off again."

"That might explain why you got far enough away for them to lose interest before running you down and finishing you off."

Jack snapped his fingers. "I just thought of something! We can also look for blood spilled on the ground."

"Yours?"

"No! I was shooting at them. Sure it was raining, but I

was also shooting at them when they tried to come at me again. I emptied a whole cylinder firing at those monsters and had to hit something."

Slocum had his doubts about that. Not only was Jack panicked, but he was most likely not using his right hand to hold his gun. His left hand would have been unfamiliar and shaky. Even under the best conditions, he doubted anyone could hit a moving target with a cobbled-together firearm like the one hanging on Jack's hip. Rather than piss on the other man's fire any more than he already had, Slocum said, "It's most likely the blood was washed away."

"Ahh. You're probably right about that. But those are the tracks! They're fresh enough, and if there were that many coyotes or wolves around here, odds are some of them would have taken a run at me between here and that town."

"Now there's a good point. Some of the tracks lead toward your camp, but others head to the east."

"You sure about that?"

"As sure as I can be. Again, you don't trust my judgment, you're more than capable of hiring someone else for the job."

"No, I trust you, John. I just didn't think we'd actually have a chance in hell of catching those things. What that animal took from me is mighty valuable. Looks like I may actually see it again."

"Don't get excited yet. We just started this ride and could lose those dogs anywhere along the way." Since his horse was already there, Slocum waited for it to stop drinking and then climbed into the saddle. "It's your ring that was swallowed, so you're the one that'll sift through any of the scat we find."

"You think it would've worked its way out so soon? I mean . . . something that size should be lodged inside of that beast for a while, right?"

Slocum shrugged. "I've learned plenty of things in my years of doing odd jobs and riding from one side of this country to the other. The time it takes for a piece of metal to work its way through a wolf's ass isn't one of them."

"All right, then. I'll do the dirty work." Jack climbed into his saddle, which was much more of an ordeal than it had been for Slocum. Although, considering it had been less than a day since his fingers had gone missing, he seemed to be compensating for them pretty well.

"You sure you're up for this?" Slocum asked. "You're looking a little green around the gills."

Jack started to nod, wavered for a moment, leaned over to vomit, but only managed a few dry heaves before sitting up again. "I'm fine. Don't ask again. Makes me think about it too much."

Slocum surveyed the terrain from the slightly higher position atop his horse. "Animals like this won't leave a steady amount of tracks for us to follow, and we don't have time to look for any if they did. Our best bet is to think ahead and figure where they might go."

"You mean . . . think like a wolf."

"More or less. Look for more watering holes or any carcasses that they might have brought down. Hopefully we can pick up their tracks somewhere along the way."

"Or catch sight of the beasts," Jack said.

"Right. Maybe we'll get lucky enough for them to catch your scent and take a run at you to finish the meal they started."

Jack lost some more of his color and choked back another dry heave. "That ain't funny."

They fanned out and rode abreast of each other so they could scour as much ground as possible. Although Slocum had started off the day skeptical as to whether he would be able to find much of anything, he found reason to hope that he might just earn his fee after all when they caught sight of an elk that had obviously been killed and partially eaten by a pack of wild animals. Tracks led away from there, where the terrain remained mostly flat in front of them. The Potrillo Mountains always seemed to be just out of reach, and every time Slocum looked at those mountains, he dreaded being led into them. He didn't have any doubt that he could safely cross the rocky slopes. It wasn't as if they were as daunting as a pass through the Rockies, but finding one pack of coyotes or wolves in them would be tough. Trying to find one before it could squeeze out a very uncomfortable piece of jewelry was damn near impossible.

If the wolf was hurting, it could make a lot of noise. But there was also the chance that it had already died and stopped leaving tracks.

It was later in the afternoon when the sun's rays hit the ground at an angle that bounced perfectly off several spots on the desert floor, causing them to glimmer like mirrors embedded in the earth. Before he lost sight of them, Slocum signaled to Jack and pointed them out. "Looks like more watering holes," he said. "You take a look at the ones over there, and I'll take these closer to me."

Jack waved excitedly and rode toward the spots. It wasn't long before the angle of the sun no longer hit the puddles just right, but they were fairly close together and Slocum found almost all of the ones he'd been after. Unfortunately, the ground around them was either solid rock or too muddy to hold a print. An exasperated sigh was still leaking out of him when Slocum heard a sound from the opposite end of the emotional spectrum.

"John! Come over here! I found something!"

Slocum rushed over to where Jack was standing. Despite his haste, he still thought the other man might jump out of his skin before he arrived. "What is it?" he asked.

Jabbing a finger down to the ground, Jack exclaimed, "Look right there! Look at them tracks and tell me they ain't the same ones we saw by the cave and that first watering hole!"

"There seems to be enough of them." After climbing

down from his horse, Slocum gazed at the imprints in the mud. "They're not as deep. That means they were left behind when the ground wasn't as wet."

"That falls in line with our timetable."

"It does."

"And to make things better, they lead in a perfect line in that direction!"

The good part was that Jack was mostly right. From what Slocum could see of the tracks, the paw prints came from the west, circled around the watering hole, and then led off to the east. The bad part was that they were headed toward the mountains.

"I think I see some watering holes further along!" Jack said. "Let's get after 'em!" He was excited enough to climb into his saddle without being tripped up too much by his wounded hand, and Slocum wasn't about to do anything to slow him down. On the contrary, he was perfectly happy to let Jack take the lead as they raced toward the next set of puddles.

Most of those puddles turned out to be anything but. Some were half-buried wagon wheels that had caught the light properly to cast a convincing reflection. Some were shiny rocks. The rest were most likely mirages drifting through the addled mind of a wounded and delirious man. No matter how many false leads he found, Jack wasn't close to losing steam. As the sunlight began to wane, he only grew more enthusiastic.

"Come on, John!" he shouted. "I see another one! Definitely more water this time!"

Slocum snapped his reins to catch up with the other man. When he did, he signaled, motioned, and finally shouted to get him to stop. As soon as he had a chance, Slocum said, "We can't go chasing every shiny thing we see!"

"Time ain't on our side," Jack replied. "For all we know, them wolves are already gone."

When Jack started to move away from him, Slocum

reached out to grab the black gelding's bridle. Fortunately for him, the horse was also tired of all that running around.

Jack turned on him with ferocity in his eyes. If he'd still had his entire right hand, he might have made a move for his pistol. "What do you think yer doin'?"

"I'm keeping you from wasting any time. How long did you stop to look at those last couple of spots? A second or two?"

"If that! How's that a waste o' time?"

"Because I can think of a dozen things you could have missed by being in such a rush," Slocum said. "If you're gonna do something half-assed, there's no point in doing it at all."

Jack sighed and nodded. "You're right. Should we go back to have another look at those first watering holes?"

Slocum let go of the other horse's bridle and settled into his saddle. When he shifted to cast reluctant eyes at the mountains, he said, "Something tells me we won't be able to do that."

"Why? Because we're runnin' out of daylight? Maybe you think we should just head into them hills?"

"We've got to consider those things. Also," he added while pointing to a ridge on one of the nearby slopes heading into a rocky wall, "there's that."

Jack turned to look at where Slocum was pointing. When he saw the row of Indians on horseback staring down at them from atop a ridge, his hand snapped to his holster. A snarled curse gurgled from the back of his throat when his right hand knocked against tooled leather.

"Yeah," Slocum said. "I agree with that sentiment."

10

Young had followed Dan's directions by cleaning up and putting on his other set of clothes. Dan couldn't decide if his altered appearance spoke more for the ability of the barber who'd trimmed Young's hair, the quality of that extra set of clothes, or the amount of dirt that was normally caked onto Young's face. Whatever it was, the difference was striking.

"So," he said to the elderly gentleman who owned the barber shop as well as rented bathtubs to anyone with fifty cents burning a hole in their pocket, "this seems like a pretty quiet town."

The barber laughed and said, "Normally, I'd say yes. Things have been fairly loud recently."

"Really? Why's that?"

"Bunch'a men charged through here this very morning." His wrinkled face scrunched into a series of deeper wrinkles as he studied Young closely. "One of them was about your size, I reckon."

Young held up his hands and grinned. "You got me. Should I walk on over to the sheriff now or after I get a splash of something to make me smell good for the ladies?"

The old man laughed and reached for a glass bottle full of his cheapest cologne. "Didn't mean to offend you, mister. Have a splash on the house. Though you won't hardly need it if you go to the Dusty Hill Saloon." He winked and said, "Just ask for Caroline. Sweet little blond thing who works there if you catch my meaning."

"I think I do. What happened with these men that charged through town?" Since he wasn't interested in a story he already knew, Young made it look as if he were listening just to let the old man get comfortable in his role as storyteller. When the barber paused to take a breath, Young asked, "Was one of those men named Jack Halsey?"

"Don't know if I caught any names. I bet the sheriff knows, but he may be kinda busy since he just got back from riding on a posse."

"You really keep abreast of current affairs."

The barber didn't have a hat, but he tapped a finger to his brow as if there was one there anyway. "Small town, you know. Anyone on Main Street saw that commotion."

"Anyone else on Main Street who might know about who came through town?"

"You just curious or are you a friend of this Halsey fellow?"

"I'm a writer," Young said with complete confidence that only a writer or a very good liar could attach to that statement. "Been riding through the territory looking for something worth selling to a newspaper. You point me in the right direction and I'll be sure you get credit for it."

"In print?"

"Yes, sir."

"Mention my shop as well?"

"In black and white," Young assured him.

"There was a fella who rode with the sheriff on that posse. Name's Slocum, I believe. He was stayin' at the Dusty Hill Saloon with one of the girls that works there. If he ain't available to answer your questions, he may have spoken to someone else. Sheriff Reyes is pretty tight-lipped about official business."

"Sounds like you know from experience."

"Like I said before," the barber replied. "Small town. Only news we get is what we can dredge up on our own. Fact is, I already been pestering the sheriff about what happened with the commotion and such, and if I pester him any more, he's likely to get sore. A man in my position can't afford to lose customers. Maybe you should just ask Dale at the saloon. Between him and those girls of his, there's always someone watching what goes on around here."

"Ain't that always the case? Should have started there anyhow." That was the truth, and if it hadn't been for his need of a change in appearance, Young would have walked straight into the saloon to ask his questions.

"Will I still get that mention in print?"

"Yes, sir."

It was only a matter of minutes before Young found himself in the Dusty Hill Saloon speaking to a sweet little blonde named Caroline. She wore a dark red dress that hugged her ample curves. A bright smile was framed by flowing gold hair. She obviously knew what she was doing when she brightened her smile even more, but Young kept his focus.

"I've heard of Jack Halsey," she said. "One of the other girls here was staying with the man who rode with the sheriff and he told her all about him."

"Did he mention where Jack's staying?"

"I don't know about that."

"What about the man who rode with the sheriff?" Young asked. "What's his name?"

She straightened up like a little girl who was proud to know the answer of a question posed by her favorite school teacher. The gesture caused her bosom to swell beneath the constraints of her corset as she replied, "John Slocum."

"Maybe I should talk to this friend of yours. I really need to find Jack Halsey."

"Last I saw him, he was with Mr. Slocum. They left town."

"Where did they go?"

"I don't know, but my friend does. I could ask her for you and then tell you everything she said."

There was no question that there was a price attached to those actions. A woman in her line of work knew ten different ways to ask for money from a man, and they were all set up by a pretty smile and a lingering glimpse at pale cleavage or the flutter of eyelashes. Caroline showed him all of those things, and he was having a difficult time trying to find fault in it. "Why can't I just talk to her?" he asked.

"Because she doesn't know you," Caroline said while stepping up close and running her fingertips along Young's chest. Even though they stood at the corner of a bar in the middle of a saloon with just under half a dozen people inside, she had a way of making him feel as if they were alone in the most intimate of ways. "She knows me and will tell me things she wouldn't tell you if you asked her the same questions."

"How much will that cost me?"

"Ten dollars."

In all honesty, Young had already found most of what he was after. There were probably plenty of reasons for him to hurry up and get back to Dan and Karl before this Jack Halsey fellow got away, but he couldn't think of them while Caroline was pressing herself against him. In fact, he was having a hard time thinking of anything other than the soft little hand that was sliding over his belt buckle to brush against the front of his jeans.

"What will I get for twenty?" he asked while waving the bills in front of her.

* * *

Ten minutes later, he was in a room on the second floor of the saloon, stripped naked, and lying on his back. Caroline's dress was on the floor, leaving her in nothing but black boots that laced all the way up to her knees. Her body was something out of a dream and felt even softer than he could have imagined when she climbed on top of him and straddled his hips. She smiled wide, reached between his legs, and stroked his cock until it was hard as stone.

"What did . . . you find out?" he asked.

"John Slocum is the name of the man who rode with Sheriff Reyes. He stopped by to collect his things and told her he was headed east with Jack Halsey."

"East, huh?" Young asked, trying to make it seem like he was in charge of at least some of his faculties.

She didn't buy the act for a moment. "That's right," she said while opening her legs so she could hold his cock steady while grinding her wet pussy against it. "Jack's wounded. He may need a doctor, so that may slow them down. Mr. Slocum seemed to think they were headed into the Potrillos sooner or later."

"I'll have to ride hard to catch up to him, then. Probably shouldn't stay here for too long."

Caroline shifted herself forward and guided him into her. "Well then. I should ride hard, too, I suppose."

Before he could say another word, Caroline lowered herself onto him and leaned forward to place her hands flat upon his chest. She rocked back and forth while pumping her hips insistently. Every time she took all of him inside, she let out a soft, contented sigh. Young reached out to grab on to her hips. They were smooth and warm against his palms, but her breasts felt even better when he cupped them in his hands. Whenever he pumped up into her, he felt her entire body respond. She even straightened her back in a way similar to how she'd caught his interest downstairs and clasped her hands over his to keep them in place as she rode him faster.

Young rubbed her hips and legs. She kept her hands on her breasts and even started rubbing them as if to make up for what she was missing now that his touch had wandered elsewhere. He thought about reaching for her again, but was enjoying himself too much just by watching her. Caroline's eyes were closed as she continued to massage herself. One of her hands remained pressed against a supple breast while another drifted between her legs. As she rode him slower, she began to rub the sensitive nub of flesh just above the spot where he entered her. Soon, Young felt her hand guiding his to that same spot.

"Here you go," she whispered. "Right there. Nice and soft."

The lips of her pussy were warm and moist as they glided up and down along his shaft. The spot where she urged him to touch her was even softer, and when his fingers found her clit, Caroline's entire body trembled.

"Don't stop," she cried. "Don't stop."

He kept rubbing her until she clenched her eyes shut and tensed every muscle below her waist. When her climax passed, she opened her eyes and looked down at him as if he were a piece of raw meat. Young was taken aback for a second, but wasn't about to protest as she picked up her pace once more. Caroline arched her back and slid her fingers through her hair while grinding her hips furiously against his. Every inch of his cock was driven into her again and again. Her breasts swayed as she built to a powerful rhythm. It was all Young could do to hang on and keep from being shoved off the bed as he grabbed on to her hips and thrust into her.

"Give it to me," she cried. "Harder!"

Young had never had a woman take control that way and had certainly never had one talk to him like that. Just feeling her muscles tense beneath her skin as she rode him was enough to send him over the edge. His instincts told his body what to do, and soon he felt as if the rest of him was merely along for the ride.

Every time he pulled out of her, he ached to be inside again.

When he buried his cock between her legs, he couldn't go deep enough.

The scent of Caroline's skin and hair enveloped him. Her flesh had built up a sheen of sweat that made her naked body glisten in the light trickling in through the window. As if sensing how close he was, she took every inch of him into her and moved her hips in quick circles. At the perfect time, she pumped back and forth until he exploded inside her.

"God *damn*!" Young shouted.

She slowed like a toy that had wound all the way down. Leaning forward to lie on top of him, Caroline wriggled while using her hands to prop her head less than an inch above his face. "I take it that was worth your twenty dollars?"

His hands wandered along her hips and lingered on the curve of her ass. "Y . . . yes."

"Good," she said while climbing off him. "Then I'll let you be on your way. Wouldn't want your friend to get too far ahead of you."

"Friend?"

"You know? Jack Halsey?"

"Right. Jack Halsey."

He watched as she pulled on her dress and cinched herself into it. This wasn't the first time he'd been with a whore. Those other times, he'd paid a lot less for a hell of a lot more time. Still, Caroline had a way of standing with her body displayed for him just right, squirming into her dress and primping herself as if it was all not only a show, but a show he would gladly pay to see again. He wanted to protest before she left him in that room. Wanted to demand some of his money back or at least some more of her time, but didn't have the strength to stop her before she blew him a kiss and pranced out of the room.

Young found his second wind by the time he'd gotten dressed and stormed outside. There was a shapely woman with dark hair farther down the hall who cast a knowing smile in his direction while walking toward the stairs.

"Where's Caroline?" he asked.

"Don't know. Should I give her your best?"

Sighing, but not regretting the money he spent, Young said, "Yeah. You do that."

Dan and Karl had made camp in roughly the same spot as Jack when he'd been bitten. Having found the ring of rocks where the fire had been made, they built another one so they could warm their hands as the sun's glow faded from the desert sky. It was a bone-dry chill that sliced through flesh quicker than a wedge of sharpened steel. Since it would save a lot of work if Jack Halsey was close enough to spot the blaze and come sniffing around his old camp, Dan stoked the fire good and high. When he saw the rider approach from the direction of Rocas Rojas, he remained seated with his hands outstretched toward the crackling flames and waited for the rider to approach and dismount.

"You were gone long enough," Karl said as he shifted upon a pile of flat stones. "Better have done more than have a few drinks and a shave."

"I sure did," Young said.

"Wipe that fuckin' smile off yer face and give me a reason why I don't fill a hole in this desert with a freshly scrubbed corpse."

Young obliged on both counts, telling him everything he'd learned while in town. Even though he'd found out more than enough to complete the task he'd been given, he couldn't help wondering if he was still about to be dropped into the grave Dan had mentioned.

"You're sure about all of that?" Dan asked.

"You told me to ask around in that town and that's what I heard. That ain't good enough, then you can go ask yourself." Although he'd attempted to make his voice sound imposing, Young knew he'd failed to impress.

"We found some tracks leading away from here. They lead to some rocks and then strike out to the east," Dan said. "You reckon that's them?"

"Two sets of tracks?"

Dan nodded.

"That's gotta be them! What the hell are we wasting time here for? Let's get a move on!"

Dan got to his feet and walked over to his horse. "Speaking of wasting time, if you fed me some bad information just to cover your ass, you'll owe me the money I lost in letting this man get away."

"Part of that money's mine, too," Young said. "I ain't workin' for free."

"What about Oklahoma Bill? Did you catch sight of him?"

"No. Everything I heard said he was still locked up at the sheriff's office. Probably waiting for a judge to conduct a trial."

"And you're sure nobody there knew who you was or who you were riding with?"

"Hell no, Dan. It was just like you said. Anyone who saw us was either too scared to look at my face real close or didn't recognize me with my hair and clothes changed."

"You're sure about that? Because I've heard of John Slocum, and if he knows we're comin', this job could be a lot harder."

"Trust me. If that sheriff knew about me or if anyone told him, he would've taken a run at me while I was in town." Young knew that for certain because even a one-legged lawman would have been able to climb the stairs quickly enough to get the drop on him while he was pinned between

Caroline's legs. Of course, there was no reason to share that little bit of insight with Dan.

Going strictly by the scowl on Dan's face, he already had a pretty good idea of what had occupied so much of Young's time while he was in town. "All right, then. Stay on that horse because we've still got some riding to do."

"Now?" Karl asked. "It'll be dark soon."

"Can you still see the ground?"

"Yeah."

"Then you can see the tracks we already found."

"He's right, Dan," Young said. "There's a lot out here that can trip a horse up. Could be dangerous to ride much more than a mile or two."

"You don't have to tell me that. I been tracking since before you was born." Shifting his attention back and forth between both other men, he added, "I know you men did plenty of work for Bill. He may have pulled in some good hauls, but he paid more attention to appearances and establishing a name for himself than doing a job properly."

"Yeah," Karl chuckled. "What kinda name is Oklahoma Bill anyhow?"

Completely disregarding Karl, Young said, "Bill was good for more than that. Plenty of people know his name, and that goes a long way no matter what sort of job it is that needs doing."

"And it landed him in jail," Dan said. "You know how many lawmen in Texas alone have heard of Oklahoma Bill Dressel? Enough to start a cattle drive. You know how many have heard of me? Five. Two of them are you, one is in jail, and the others are dead. You want to follow Bill and do things his way? March back into Rocas Rojas and turn yourself in to that sheriff. You want to follow me? Shut your damn mouths and ride. Now that we know we're after the right man and that he did come back this way on his way to the Potrillos, we'll follow the tracks we found and look for a campfire. Before first light, we ride to catch up to this man.

We also know John Slocum is with him. He's a killer, so be ready for a fight. Long as we know who we're up against, what they're after, and which way they're headed, we got an edge."

"You think that Italian fella is good for what he offered for this job?" Karl asked.

The smirk on Dan's face was as rare as it was ugly. "He's desperate to get whatever Halsey is carrying. He'll either pay us double what he offered to get it, or we take it and cash it in for ourselves. Either way, we win."

After that, all three men were ready to ride.

11

The Indians that had found them were Apache. Slocum could tell as much by the war paint on their faces, the way they handled their weapons, and the minimal amount of gear they had on their horses. Also, there was a silent ferocity that every Apache warrior possessed at birth that took most men a lifetime to acquire. Every one of the seven men escorting Slocum and Jack through the narrow mountain pass had that fierce look in his eyes. Jack was doing a good job of maintaining his composure, but it was clear he had the same concern as Slocum regarding their odds of making it out of those mountains alive.

"We didn't try to fight you," Slocum said.

None of the warriors responded. They'd descended like a rockslide, pouring down from higher ground on all sides. Arrows were notched in the bows of more riders who remained up high while the seven came down to collect them wielding tomahawks and thick clubs capped with stone. Some called those the weapons of barbarians. Slocum knew better than to write them off so easily. Mostly because the men who scoffed at Apache warriors had either never met one or died regretting their mistake.

Although Jack cast his eyes wildly in every direction, Slocum had his fixed upon the warrior who rode at the front of the formation.

"They didn't take our weapons," Jack whispered.

"I know. We'll leave them right where they are."

"But what do they want?"

"We'll find out soon enough," Slocum replied.

"Or they'll kill us soon enough."

"If they wanted to kill us, they would have done it already."

"Your leader is right," the Apache at the front of the group said.

"He ain't my leader," Jack said.

Some of the Apaches spoke to each other in their own language. Judging by their tone, they were mildly amused by Jack's attempt at a stern demeanor.

"Perhaps he should lead you," the head Apache said. "Then he could tell you when to be silent."

"Jack," Slocum said. "Shut the hell up."

The head Apache shifted in his saddle just enough to get a look at Slocum. "A leader who also knows when to follow. That is rare."

"Not following," Slocum replied. "Just wanting him to shut the hell up."

Most of the Apache chuckled at that. The ones who didn't only had to wait for Slocum's words to be translated into their language. Then they laughed.

"Well, I'm glad you all find this so damned amusing," Jack said. "I for one don't . . ." He stopped himself short when he looked over to Slocum and saw the deadly glare that was pointed in his direction.

"My loud friend is right," Slocum said. "You didn't take our weapons and didn't bind our hands."

"I could change that if you like," the head Apache said.

"That's not necessary. Does make me wonder what you're after, though."

The Apache at the front of the line stared straight ahead, and all the others behind him lost every bit of expression that had previously been on their faces. For the moment, it seemed the men had become just another cluster of rocks within the mountain pass.

Finally, Jack lost what little composure he still had. "We can get out of this, John. What the hell else am I payin' you for? And *don't* tell me to shut up again!"

"You make one move toward your gun and you're on your own. Do you understand me?" When Jack started to say something, Slocum snapped, "Do you understand?"

Rather than speak, Jack settled into his saddle and cradled his hand as if it had suddenly started hurting again. That wasn't an unreasonable thing, considering the scant amount of medical attention he'd received.

Slocum was grateful if the wound caused the other man to sulk on his own for a while. To the head Apache, he said, "We're not going to harm anyone. That's not why we're here."

The Apache brought his men to a halt by extending a hand to one side as if he were chopping into the side of a rock face. "We know that now," he said.

"Then there's no reason to keep us any longer."

Bringing his horse around with a few subtle pulls of the hand that was embedded within the animal's mane, the Apache leader turned to face Slocum as if he and the horse shared a heartbeat. "I think there is."

For a moment, Slocum considered going back on his own command. The muscles in his gun arm twitched in response to the intent glare etched into the Indian's features. If he was going to make a stand against the Apache, there was no good time for it. Taking his chances here and now seemed a hell of a lot more appealing than waiting for the archers who'd stayed in the higher rocks to come along. "What reason would that be?" he asked.

"That man is wounded. He bleeds."

Shoving his bandaged hand under his left arm, Jack said, "Ain't nothin' that could keep me from defendin' myself!"

Sparing only the quickest glance to Jack, the Apache looked back to Slocum and said, "The animals you seek can smell the blood."

"What animals?" Slocum asked.

"Cha'to." Since that didn't register immediately with either of the two men, the Apache placed his hand flat upon his nose, tapped it, and said, "The wolf with the flat snout. We know you are hunting him."

"How the hell could you know that?" Jack asked.

One of the Apache riding closest to Jack scoffed and said, "We have followed you for miles. You speak so loudly of the wolf that took your hand that deaf women three towns away must have heard you."

"You were following us?"

"You are trespassing on our land," the Apache leader said. "We go where we please."

"If we're such invaders, then why not kill us?" Slocum asked. Knowing Jack was about to jump out of his skin without so much as looking at the other man, Slocum held him back with a warning hand. "Instead you lead us through this pass without bothering to take our weapons."

"If you are after Cha'to, then perhaps we need to help each other. That wolf is an eater of men."

Suddenly, Jack brightened up. "See?" he declared victoriously. "I told you so! I told you that damn thing was a menace!"

"Yeah, Jack," Slocum said. "You know so much, so why don't you take it from here?" When Jack eased back into his saddle, Slocum looked back to the Apache leader. "What do you want from us?"

"First, we needed to see if you were on our land to spill our blood. We see that you are not. We also want you to see that if you did think about making war with my people, you would be making a mistake."

"Wouldn't be the first time," Slocum said while casting his eyes in Jack's direction.

"Cha'to has been gathering a pack. We have seen wolves in these mountains, but they have been rare for many seasons. Some among us think the spirit world is making warriors to inflict pain on the white invaders. Perhaps this is the case."

Jack pulled his hand from where it had been lodged under his arm and placed it casually on his knee as if his wounds had suddenly healed themselves. The wince that drifted across his face when his bandages knocked against his leg was almost subtle enough for him to cover. Almost, but not quite.

"Have any of your people been hurt?" Slocum asked.

The Apache fell silent for a few seconds. The tension in the air was unmistakably that of men who had fresh wounds of their own. Breaking the silence with a steady voice, the head Apache said, "One of our women and two of our children were killed by the pack you seek. Many of our warriors have sacrificed their flesh to the hunt."

"Are you certain it's the same pack we're after?" Jack asked anxiously.

Without batting an eye, the Apache told him, "If you wish to hunt with us as free men or ride as slaves, you will hunt the same pack as we do."

Jack nodded once. "Sounds fair enough."

Everyone seemed to be taken aback when Slocum proved to be the one who wasn't going to go quietly any longer. "The hell it does," he said.

The Apache at the head of the group furrowed his brow and said, "You are in no position to defy us."

"Just because you can listen to this one talk from a distance doesn't mean you earned our respect. And just because you act like civilized men doesn't mean you got any favors coming to you."

Either responding to a touch of the Apache's hand or a tap of his knee against its sides, the Indian's horse ambled forward until the Apache was close enough to swipe at him with one of the many sharpened weapons carried on his person. "I thought you were a man who could be reasoned with."

"I am."

"Then why do you speak to me this way?"

Keeping his chin up and his back straight, Slocum spoke as if he had an entire army behind him. "We are after a pack of wolves and we could sure use any bit of help that's being offered. Both of us stand to gain from killing those animals, but it seems your people will gain just a bit more."

"How so?"

"Several of you were hurt, but it's just my friend and I on this hunt. So far, he's the only one with a scratch to show for it."

"That can change very quickly." It was clear by the edge in his voice that the Apache leader was talking about more than the wolves being a threat. To his credit, he did have men to back him up. "Half of your number have spilled their blood," he added in a somewhat less threatening tone. "Our losses aren't nearly so bad."

"I guess it all depends on how you look at it."

The Indian riding alongside Jack's horse tightened his grip on his weapon, which was one of the clubs fashioned from a thick length of wood with a flat rock tied to one end. It was a simple weapon, but had enough chips and dark stains on it to show it had inflicted more than its share of damage. "I told you we should not expect help from white men!" he snarled.

Some of the others voiced their agreement. The more the Apaches spoke, the more they drifted into their own language. Even the leader abandoned his well-crafted English in favor of the more comfortable dialect which he'd known since birth.

At one point, Jack shot a quick glance at Slocum while tensing ever so slightly to let him know he was ready to fight. The Apache were arguing heatedly among themselves, which meant most of them were too involved to be as focused on them as they had throughout the rest of the ride. Slocum returned Jack's look with one of his own that pinned the wounded man in place.

It hadn't seemed like a very long ride from the point where they'd first crossed paths with the Indians, but they'd easily gone for a few miles into the slopes of the Potrillo Mountains. Slocum wasn't too familiar with that particular trail to begin with, and he doubted the Apache were using a trail that was known to anyone outside of their tribe. And even if they could get away from their escort with a minimum of fuss, there was still the second group with bows to think about. All of that flashed through Slocum's mind in a rush, convincing him that now was not the time to make any sudden moves.

Jack clenched his jaw and winced as the muscles in his gun hand flexed. He wasn't happy about it, but he'd apparently come to the same conclusion.

Finally, the leader of the Apaches lifted himself up an inch or so from his horse and held his tomahawk over his head. The gesture was meant either to quiet his men or to make sure Slocum and Jack didn't get any ideas. By displaying the deadly weapon and letting out a sharp cry, he accomplished both tasks.

The other Apache didn't cower in front of their leader, but they held their tongues and didn't make a move to challenge him.

Jack was nervous as Slocum showed him a single nod. It wasn't very reassuring given their circumstances, but it was the best he could manage at that time.

"My men don't want to trust you," the Apache leader said. "And I am having doubts as well."

"I have doubts, too," Slocum said. "Especially since you and your men jumped us and forced us to come this way like we didn't have a say in the matter. You want to know why white men call you savages? Incidents like this one right here."

"You still have your weapons," the Apache closest to Jack said. "Use them!"

The leader hissed a warning in his own language, which didn't do a thing to erase the challenging glint from the other Indian's eye.

"Your hands are not bound," that Indian said. "Challenge us if that's what you want."

Slocum took stock of the men around him in much the same way he would evaluate opponents sitting at a card table. From what he could gather, the Apache were ready to call damn near any bluff that was set in front of them. A few were itching for the chance to do so. Rather than give them a reason to clean him out, Slocum said, "We could have done that at any time. In fact, I'm not in the habit of allowing myself to be led around this way."

"You hold yourself like a warrior," the Apache leader said. "And you seem to have more sense than most white men, who would have used their weapons to try and spill our blood. That is why you still live."

"And you strike me as men I'd rather have as allies than enemies," Slocum said. "If we're to work together, it can't be like this. Tracking anything isn't easy. Tracking a pack of wolves in these rocks is even harder. Trying to do that while we're questioning each other every step of the way is damn near impossible. I understand you don't have any reason to hold us in too high regard, but the least we deserve is some common courtesy."

The Apache leader's eyes narrowed, but not in a way that could be construed as aggressive. Instead, he seemed to be studying Slocum as he said, "You have been hunting Cha'to. So have we. Together, we can find him and his pack before any more blood is spilled."

Slocum nodded. "Agreed."

Jack nodded even harder and reached out to pat the closest Apache on the arm. "And who said you fellas were savages?"

The Indian scowled at Jack and then looked down to scowl even harder at Jack's hand.

Retracting his arm as if it had been set on fire, Jack said, "Forget I mentioned that word. Thanks for not killin' us, by the way. Very civilized of you. Honestly."

"Jack," Slocum said, "shut the hell up."

12

The Apache were camped in a narrow gulley formed by a
ridge on one side and the steeper rocky slope of the Potrillos on the other. Slocum had seen plenty of Indian settle-
ments, and this one had the looks of one that was meant to
be torn down and moved at a moment's notice. The tents
were hastily raised and barely looked large enough for a
pair of warm bodies to be sheltered during the night. There
was no fire being tended. Even the horses were clustered
together with blankets still on their backs as if they would
be mounted and ridden at a full gallop at any second.

"Strange," Jack said as he leaned over to speak in a
coarse whisper. "Don't see any women."

"What were you expecting?" Slocum asked. "Dancing
girls?"

"No, but there should be a few women doing chores or
whatever squaw women do." Noticing the stern glare from
one of the nearby Apaches, Jack lowered his voice even
further and leaned toward Slocum at such an angle that put
him in danger of falling from his saddle. "Best not call 'em
squaws, I guess."

Slocum had already gotten used to blocking out the sound of Jack's voice. In the short amount of time he'd known him, it was the only way to keep from adding to the wounded man's list of injuries. Unlike those other times when he was flapping his gums without much of a point, Jack actually made some sense.

There were a few younger Apache filling water skins or preparing a freshly killed bit of game, but all were males. The air was heavy with purpose, and every eye was trained upon the new arrivals.

"There ain't no children either," Jack pointed out.

"I noticed that."

"What do you think that means?"

Noticing the head Apache had signaled for the others to stop and was swinging down from his horse, Slocum said, "Looks like we're about to find out."

Now that he was off his horse, the Apache who'd proved to be the leader of the party that had surrounded Slocum and Jack was taller than Slocum had originally thought. His torso was lean at the waist and widened as it flowed upward into broad shoulders. He wore a tanned leather tunic that Slocum could now see was decorated with elaborate designs of beads as well as colors that had been painted on. It wasn't until now that Slocum had seen the Apache leader straight-on. Before, the other man had either been turning to look at him from an angle or had been too far away for him to get a good look. Also, Slocum had been more concerned with survival to notice details such as clothing.

Now that he was convinced the Apache didn't want them dead just yet, Slocum soaked up as many details as he could. If he had to, he could get from the camp back to the spot where they'd been captured—he could do it with his eyes closed. He'd also become aware that the rest of the ambushers were still shadowing them from higher ground. Every now and then throughout the ride to the camp, he'd spotted figures darting along a ridge or heard the scrape of an errant hoof slipping on some loose gravel. Wherever the Apache archers were, they would know if any false move had been made and would surely put an end to those moves with several well-placed arrows. Slocum was distracted by those thoughts when he heard the sound of horses in the distance breathing heavily as if from a hard ride. He glanced up at a series of ridges looking down at the camp on the mountain side, but the angle of the sun covered those rocks in thick shadow.

"Come," the Apache leader said. "Join us in a meal. Have some water."

"We got our own water," Jack said.

"But," Slocum added while climbing down from his saddle, "it's neighborly of you to offer us some of yours. Ain't that right, Jack?"

Grudgingly, Jack went through the arduous process of dismounting. "Sure," he said. "Let's just sit and have a nice long talk while them wolves run to hell and back."

"As long as they come back, what is the reason to complain?" another Apache asked.

"I think he's got you there," Slocum said.

Since he wasn't about to spell out his reasons for wanting those wolves as soon as he could find them, Jack muttered to himself and walked over to join Slocum near the ashen pile marking a spot where a cooking fire had been.

The Apache leader squatted down next to the fire pit so he could pull aside a pelt that had been lying on the ground. Beneath it were several strips of lean meat that had shriveled around narrow spits. He picked up one of the spits, pulled off a chunk of meat with his teeth, and began chewing the leathery snack. He then held the pelt up a little higher as an informal invitation for his guests to partake. Slocum took a spit and offered one to Jack. When the wounded man turned his nose up at it, Slocum slapped one against his chest until he took it anyway.

"I am called Snake Catcher," the Apache leader said. "I

know your name is John because this one has mentioned it many times."

"John Slocum," he said while extending his hand. It was shaken by Snake Catcher, strongly yet reluctantly. "And this is Jack Halsey."

"How about you tell my name to everyone you meet?" Jack groused. "There are still men after me, you know."

"We know."

Until those two words were spoken, Slocum hadn't realized there were men climbing down from the ridge to enter the camp. Considering they were the same archers that he'd been looking for only a few moments ago, their stealthy appearance was quite a feat. There were only three of them, which meant either that more were hidden and waiting for the white men to slip up or that the group had covered enough ground to seem larger. From what Slocum knew about the Apache warriors, either choice was just as likely to be true.

Not shaken by the archers coming down from the rocks, Jack wheeled around to ask them, "What do you mean you know? What do you know?"

"There were men riding from the same direction you came," one of the archers said. He was shorter than most of the Apache, had long coal black hair and eyes that were so narrow they looked more like slits that had been cut into the sand-blasted surface of his face. "They stopped to look at the ground, searching for something, then riding after you."

"Tracking us," Slocum said.

The short archer nodded once and approached the fire pit to help himself to some of the tough meat.

"Well, that's just great!" Jack said.

Snake Catcher bared his teeth while chewing. "This one talks too loud. Like an impatient child."

"Speaking of children," Slocum said. "Where are the ones in your tribe? I don't see any around here."

"Them or women," Jack added.

"You are interested in our women?" the short archer asked.

Before Jack could put his foot into his mouth yet again, Slocum said, "No, we're not. Just making an observation."

"Flying Spear is suspicious of all white men," Snake Catcher said. "And they have reason to be suspicious of him."

Driving the end of his longbow into the ground as if he were planting a flag, Flying Spear said, "I have scalped many and still I go where I please. To your people, I am a ghost."

"Anyone who believes in ghosts ought to be scalped," Jack replied.

For a moment, the Apache were silent. Then, as Snake Catcher and Flying Spear traded a few glances, they started to laugh. Some of the others in the camp chuckled, but not all were amused. For the moment, however, some of the tension in the air seemed to have been depleted.

"This is not a home," Snake Catcher said. "This is just a place to rest our horses and our heads until Cha'to is captured."

Sneering directly into Jack's face, Flying Spear said, "We bring the beasts to us. Perhaps they come when we are sleeping. Or perhaps we draw them here with the scent of freshly spilled blood."

"If all you needed was bait," Slocum said, "you could have gutted us and spread us out on open ground."

While Jack may not have taken any comfort from that observation, Snake Catcher nodded sagely and said, "My words to you are true. If you try to take advantage of our offer at peace, then we will use you for the bait we need."

"Temporary peace," Flying Spear added.

"And what happens after the wolves are killed?" Slocum asked.

Snake Catcher gnawed on the leathery meat and then placed his spit into the dirt beside the pelt. "Maybe we take your scalps and sell them. You know that there are plenty of white men looking for such things."

"And since there are men with guns looking for you already," Flying Spear added, "we know where to go to sell them."

"Not a very good way to forge a partnership," Slocum said.

Sitting with his legs bent and his arms propped on his knees, Snake Catcher said, "If you prove to be good partners, we will treat you as allies. Try to cheat us or take what we have . . ."

"You found us, remember? We're not out to cheat anyone and we don't know what you have. This ain't even your main camp." When the Apache nodded in agreement, Slocum continued. "My friend here could use some medicine. Do you have anything to help with that?"

"His hand?"

"That's right. Show him, Jack."

Always anxious to get attention for his impressive wounds, Jack unwound the bandages and peeled away the blood-soaked cloths beneath them. His hand and the tips of his fingers looked as if they'd been dipped into dark red clay that had turned into a flaky crust. Even though his arm and elbow seemed fine, he grunted dramatically when he extended his arm so the Apache could get a better look.

The Indians took an interest in the wounds, but a minimum of emotion could be seen on their dark, stoic faces. "This was done by Cha'to?" Snake Catcher asked.

"Damn right," Jack replied. "Chewed 'em right off faster than you ate that damn meat on a stick you all seem to like so much."

"You are lucky. You should see what was left of our people that were attacked."

"We're all lucky to have joined up this way," Slocum said. "And we'd be even luckier if you could help out my friend here with his wounds."

"There is a healer among our tribe. He is an old man who must stay with the women and children, but if you prove worthy of his medicine, we will take you to him."

"Don't you got anything for pain?" Jack asked. "What would happen if one of you broke an arm or got bit yourselves?"

Flying Spear had cleaned all of the meat from one of the spits and tossed it toward the pelt with a flick of his wrist. It stuck in the ground with enough force to have pinned the tanned skin into place if that had been his intention. "We wear our scars proudly and use our pain like fire in our souls."

"Real goddamn poetic."

Thankfully, Snake Catcher found some amusement in Jack's never-ending bellyaching. "You have made it this far with your pain. You can ride a little farther. If not, you're of no use to us."

That put an end to Jack's whining for the moment. Glad for the respite, Slocum said, "So you've got our help. When do you want to start the hunt?"

"As long as those beasts are alive, the hunt will never stop," Flying Spear said.

"He is one who lost someone to Cha'to," Snake Catcher explained. "One of many. He is anxious to spill the blood of that one and the entire pack onto the ground."

"Him and me both!" Jack said while flapping his mangled hand for emphasis.

Looking at Slocum, the Apache leader said, "It is dark. If Cha'to is near, we will hear his cry. Sometimes, he is even louder than your friend."

"Hard to believe," Slocum muttered.

"Some of our warriors are watching for Cha'to, listening for his cry. If he shows himself this night, we will find him and the beasts that follow him. Until then, we rest and prepare for the battle."

Slocum turned to look behind him where the horses

were kept. Since his stallion and Jack's gelding were being fed and watered along with the rest of them, he let them be. For the moment, none of the Apaches seemed interested in going through their saddlebags. That wasn't much of a surprise. If they were interested in looting, there would be plenty of time for that after the bodies hit the dirt.

Slocum dozed for an hour or two, but did so with one eye open. It allowed him to put some wind back into his sails, but was far from what he might consider restful. When he awoke, he checked the watch in his pocket to find he'd actually slept a bit longer than he'd thought. The camp was the same as when he'd left it, which meant his open eye hadn't missed much of anything after all. He sat up, got to his feet, and took a few steps toward the perimeter of the camp. There were a few Apache sitting in the shadows, sharpening knives or preparing arrows, but none of them did anything more than watch him go by. At one edge of the camp, the walls enclosing the site opened to the top of a drop-off that was no less than twenty or thirty feet above the desert floor. He still had yet to hear so much as a word of warning from the Apache, but Slocum decided to stay put rather than push his luck with what might be mistaken for an escape attempt.

In the quiet of the night, the scrambling steps approaching Slocum from behind might as well have been nails raking across a piece of dry slate. "What were you gonna do?" Jack asked breathlessly after coming to a stop beside him. "Leave without me?"

"Wasn't going anywhere," Slocum said. "Just getting a breath of fresh air."

"Fresh air's all we got out here. Sure as hell ain't about to get a damn bed or blanket."

"If you need a blanket so badly, take one from the horses."

"Very funny. I think we might be able to get away if we can distract them Injuns by the tents."

"Those are the only ones you saw? Jesus, you really do need someone to ride with you to get anything done."

"All right then, smart aleck," Jack snapped. "You know so much, then tell me what we should do to get out of this."

"Why get out of it? These men want the same thing we do. How many packs of bloodthirsty wolves can be along this same path we've been on? So far, I don't see a reason why we shouldn't help them. Besides, you could use some attention for that hand. It's not looking so good."

"What do you mean?" Jack asked as he lifted his hand and twisted it back and forth as if looking for a mole. "It ain't no worse than it was before."

"How does it feel?"

"Actually, not too bad. I been playin' it up a little from time to time."

"Really?" Slocum scoffed. "I wouldn't have guessed. But just because it's not giving you a fit don't mean it's good. You should be able to feel more pain than you do. Considering how much you like to whine, I'd say it must be going numb."

"Beats feeling like my damn fingers are bein' held in a fire."

"Not when it comes to losing your hand to gangrene."

"Ain't nothin' some Injun medicine man can cure."

"You'd be surprised," Slocum said. "Anyway, it couldn't hurt to get someone to look at it once we catch those wolves. That'll also give us a chance to stay around after the hunt so you can get to those animals and remove what you need from them."

"I suppose so."

Both of them looked out at a landscape bathed in pale moonlight. The stars shone overhead, only a few of which were dimmed by a thin bank of clouds being pushed by a cool breeze. Those same winds brushed against Slocum's arms, chilling him straight to the marrow in his bones. In the distance, a lone howl wavered before trailing off into a barely audible tone.

At least three Apache took positions along the ridge on that side of the camp. A few seconds after the howl fell silent, they moved away to whisper a few clipped words to one another. Slocum saw nothing but a few shadows that may or may not have been the sharp-eyed warriors making their way back to camp.

Slocum and Jack stood for a few seconds, waiting to hear any more movement or a call to action. Since the wolves had fallen silent, the Indians did the same. Even so, Slocum wasn't about to make the mistake of assuming the rest of the camp had gone to sleep.

"So you really think we can trust these men?" Jack asked.

"You're paying me to get that wolf. I think we could do a hell of a lot worse than join up with these men."

Leaning in and dropping his voice so it could barely be heard even by Slocum, Jack said, "I need more than a dead wolf."

"If we don't get a kill in the next day, I'm thinking our odds are pretty slim of finding whatever may be lodged in that animal's belly no matter what. Something tells me with this kind of help, we won't have to wait that long, though."

"And what if these Injuns ain't about to just set us loose afterwards?"

"That," Slocum replied, "is the other reason you paid me to come along."

13

Slocum must have drifted off again after the bit of commotion died down because he was awoken with a start by a howl that sounded as if it was coming from directly behind him. He sat bolt upright and reached for his gun, which was still in its holster. Flying Spear's bow creaked as an arrow was drawn back in preparation to be loosed. Its sharpened stone tip could just be seen in the predawn glow emanating from the east. Even when Slocum eased his hand away from his gun, the arrow remained notched and ready to fly.

"I think Snake Catcher made a mistake in trusting you," Flying Spear said. "Prove me right."

Getting up and dusting himself off, Slocum cleared his throat and asked, "Are we heading out after those wolves or not?"

Flying Spear's eyes narrowed. His fist tightened around the middle of his bow. The arrow drew back just a little bit more.

For a moment, Slocum thought he might actually have to draw his pistol and take his chances against an entire camp of Apaches waiting for him to make that very mistake.

Snake Catcher's voice cut through the morning haze. The archer's only response was a subtle twitch, but when the Apache leader barked at him again, Flying Spear lowered his bow.

"John Slocum is right," Snake Catcher said. "We must ride out to meet Cha'to."

Those words sent the entire camp into motion. Apache on the upper ridge waved to the men below. Both groups tossed supplies up or down at each other as the hunting party got what they needed. By the time they were ready to move, the horses had already been taken from the make-shift corral so they could be mounted and ridden away. Despite all of the commotion, one man remained as steady as the eye of a hurricane.

"What the hell's goin' on?" Jack asked as he stood up and scratched his backside. "Are we leavin'?"

Half a dozen men thundered away from the campsite into the lower expanse of the desert. Slocum and Jack were among that group, but obviously weren't the first to set out on the morning's charge. In the distance, Apache war cries sliced through the air, intermixed with the snarling baritone of what had to be several large animals. Slocum could hear the wolves barking and growling in a rage that grew as more Apache voices joined the fray.

Snake Catcher led the hunters with two men alongside him. Slocum didn't know their names, but he recognized them from the group that had brought him and Jack to the camp in the first place. He and Jack were next in line with Flying Spear and another of the archers bringing up the rear. The sun was just cresting the horizon, and the air was still cold enough to cut through Slocum's body like any one of the arrowheads that were surely poised to pierce his heart if he stepped out of line.

The air not only woke Slocum up but slapped him in the face and got the blood churning through his veins. Ears that had heard nothing but the quiet calm of sleep only moments ago were now filled with the thunder of hooves and fearsome Apache war cries. Even the sound of wolves in the distance hit him on a primal level, making him feel less like a man in a hunting party and more like a predator that could take on any number of wolves with his bare hands.

When Snake Catcher yelped in one direction, he received a response from a group of two Apache circling in from the left flank to ride ahead. Another cry was answered by three more men on horseback, who raised their bows and leaned forward over their horses' necks as if they'd become one with the powerful animals. The Indian leader raised himself up and turned as if the speed he was riding at made no difference whatsoever in what he could do along the way. He looked back at Slocum, bared his teeth, and let out another battle cry. Surprisingly enough, Jack hollered a response before Slocum could gather the breath to do so.

They didn't have far to ride before catching sight of their prey. At first, Slocum saw a cloud of dust churning about a hundred yards ahead. He squinted to try and make out what was in the middle of that swirling dirt, but the sun was making the task extremely difficult. Charging blind made Slocum's heart beat even faster, and he drew his pistol out of pure reflex.

If he had been thinking of double-crossing the Apache, now was the time. His gun was in hand, and none of the other men had a problem with it. All Slocum would have needed to do was start firing and he could have dropped at least half of the Indians before they fired back. That thought didn't even cross his mind, however. They were drawing closer to the snarling wolves, and those beasts were out for blood. Any man's blood would do. Even Jack was of that same mind since he'd had enough time to get his junk-pile pistol into his left hand without taking his eyes away from the trail ahead.

A stiff wind had blown away the dust cloud to reveal two

men on horseback and no fewer than three large wolves. Until now, Slocum still thought Jack's attackers could have been coyotes or possibly even wild dogs that may have gone rabid after running away from a ranch or farm, but there was no mistaking the size of the animals he saw. They were wolves all right. Hungry ones.

The first animal to catch his eye was a large wolf with a coat as black as a crow's wing. It reared up and swiped its paws in the air at one of the Apache warriors at the front of the hunting party. That man gripped his horse's mane tightly in one hand while swinging a tomahawk with the other. The weapon's stone blade glanced off the black wolf's shoulder, but had more of a swatting impact that knocked the animal back without doing much in the way of damage.

As soon as the black wolf rolled aside, a smaller one ran and leapt at the rider in an attempt to drag him from his saddle. Fortunately, the Apache was quick enough to tuck his tomahawk in close to his horse's side while pressing his chest flat against its mane to present less of a target. He drew his arms and legs in tight, but hadn't expected the wolf to get so much height in its leap. The smaller animal was light and had built up one hell of a head of steam, which meant it was able to snap at the warrior's upper arm in an attempt to sink its fangs into his neck.

Although he'd felt like he was flying down from the mountain before, Slocum now thought his horse was plodding through molasses. He could only watch as the smaller wolf attacked the warrior's upper body, using its paws to fight for purchase on the horse's back until a second warrior in the dust cloud got close enough to prod the wolf with the tip of a short spear. Even as the spearhead dug into its side, the wolf was hesitant to let go. By the time it did hit the ground after relinquishing its tenuous grasp, a burly gray wolf was there to renew the offensive. It and the black wolf kept their chests close to the ground and barked savagely at both horsemen. When Snake Catcher announced his presence with a sharp battle cry, the three canines turned toward the approaching hunting party and fanned out to keep all of the men in front of them.

Snake Catcher pulled back on his reins while gripping his tomahawk. In one fluid motion, he'd dropped down from his saddle, rolled away from his horse, and popped up to his feet with a look in his eyes that was almost as ferocious as the ones shown by the wolves. Although he was no stranger to being in the saddle, Slocum wasn't about to attempt to mimic the moves that the Apache seemed born to achieve. He struggled to bring his horse to a stop before turning it around and pulling away from the wolves. The pack kept low to the ground and circled to make continued attempts at bringing down the horses or tearing at the men on their backs. Slocum turned and was immediately confronted by a fourth wolf, which seemed to have been spit up from the bowels of hell.

It was larger than the other three, had a mix of brown and gray fur, and a wide face full of long teeth. It leapt up at him with saliva streaming from its mouth and wide yellow eyes blazing with a fire of their own. He didn't know how the wolf had gotten so close without being seen, but Slocum could tell this was Cha'to. Its snout truly did look as if it had been lopped off at the end to form a flat surface where the other animals' noses tapered down to sharper points. Its tongue gathered into its mouth, and every muscle in the animal's body extended to snap its head forward in a single powerful attack.

Slocum pulled back hard on his reins, causing his horse to rear up. The wolf was close enough for him to smell its fur, and Slocum reflexively pushed it back with a kick that planted his boot heel against the animal's solid chest and deflected it at the apex of its jump. A powerful breath was knocked from the wolf's body, and its jaws clamped together with enough force to do a lot more than separate a man from a few of his fingers. Fortunately, they closed on nothing but air this time.

Once the wolf was no longer about to take his head off, Slocum fired a shot with the Schofield just as a way to discourage another jumping attack. When he pulled the trigger that time and the next, he knew he wouldn't come close to hitting the ferocious animal. The instant Cha'to's paws hit the dirt, the wolf twisted to one side and scampered away. Slocum's bullets whipped through the air and sparked against rocky terrain to get him to retreat even faster.

"That's him, John!" Jack shouted. "That's the one that got me!"

Although Slocum heard those words, he wasn't about to waste time responding to them. He did his talking with the smoke wagon in his hand, sending another shot at the leader of the wolf pack.

Cha'to was a sight to behold, every move fueled by sheer aggression. Although he'd run away from Slocum, the wolf immediately set his sights on the closest horseman he could find. That search was made a whole lot easier since Jack had announced his presence with his excited voice.

"Shit! Damn! Oh God! Shit!" Jack wailed, obviously unaware of what he was saying. He fired his pistol at Cha'to, but did so in such a hurry that he would have missed even if he'd been using his right hand. As it was, his bullets didn't even get close enough to make the wolf nervous.

After taking a few scuttling steps to one side, Cha'to gathered itself up in preparation for a jump. Jack froze like a deer caught in a hunter's sights and fumbled to take another shot. Slocum wanted to fire at the wolf, but it had circled around to an angle that required him to shift in his saddle to follow. He only hoped that wouldn't give the wolf enough of an opportunity to finish the meal it had started outside Rocas Rojas.

Slocum pivoted to get the best angle possible, but it

wasn't his shot that caused the big wolf to yelp in pain. Cha'to twisted his head around and snarled while gnawing at the arrow that had been shot into his right flank. From about twenty yards away, Flying Spear shouted to one of the other archers, who'd kept their distance so they could pick their shots. More arrows hissed through the air, most of which skidded against the ground while one clipped Cha'to's hind leg.

Instead of moving slower or retreating, Cha'to snarled with even more ferocity as he turned to charge at Flying Spear. The Apache archers held their ground while notching arrows into their bows. Slocum took the opportunity to holster his Schofield and pull the Winchester from the boot in his saddle. The moment he felt the weight of the rifle in his hands, he knew it was loaded. Part of his mind was cursing for not having checked the weapon during the rush away from camp, but the rest was dedicated to the task of lining up a shot and taking it.

Once again, Cha'to surprised his human opponents by sharply turning away from them instead of committing to a wild attack. The brown and gray wolf raced toward the rest of the pack that was tussling with the Apache. Blood sprayed from the wounds in its leg and flank, which wasn't nearly enough to divert his attention from bringing the humans down.

"Stay back and shoot any of them that come at you," Slocum said to Jack.

"I ain't about to just sit here and let you do the work!"

"Then do what you please," Slocum shouted as he rode around to get a better angle on the wolves. "Just stay the hell out of our way!" He didn't ride for long before picking a spot and coming to a halt. Every second that passed without him taking a shot felt like an eternity and men were paying with their blood. Several Apache yelped in pain while others raised their voices in sharp battle cries. Both of those sounds blended together until it was difficult to figure out which men were in need of help and which were on the offensive. Drawing a long breath, Slocum steeled his nerves so he could push through the chaos and find his shot.

The smallest of the wolves leapt at Snake Catcher. He crouched while bringing his tomahawk up in a quick arc that caught the wolf's underbelly. The lean animal had yet to touch the ground again before Snake Catcher's tomahawk was snapped up and brought around again to open a wide gash along the side of the wolf's neck. The smallest of the pack was wiry and had plenty of spirit. Despite the nasty wound it had just gotten, it still seemed ready to put up a fight. Slocum snuffed the fire in that one's eyes by placing a single shot from his Winchester into the wolf's chest. The animal took another step and then crumpled, to be set upon by more tomahawk-wielding Apache.

At that moment, the gray wolf broke away from the group. Between the animals and Indians attacking each other, it was all Slocum could do to keep from firing at anything on two legs. When the gray wolf bolted, two Apache chased after it. One threw his tomahawk, but only managed to gouge the animal across its shoulder blade. As if sensing the Apache was without a weapon, the gray wolf stopped and turned around to face him with its teeth bared. Although the Apache tried to hop to one side in an erratic change of direction, he wasn't able to outsmart the wolf. It clawed at the ground and spoke in a series of haggard barks rivaling the Apache's war cry. One of the hunter's feet skidded on a patch of gravel, sending him to the ground and the wolf wasted no time before pouncing on him.

There were other Apache in the vicinity, but none were able to dissuade the wolf once it had fresh blood splashing on its tongue. The weaponless Apache screamed more in a rage than in pain, but was ripped apart all the same. Two more warriors descended on the wolf, driving spears and tomahawks into its torso. Even as the ground beneath the wolf became slick with blood, the animal continued to fight. One of the Apache staggered away, clutching a rough gash in his arm before the gray wolf finally stopped moving.

When Slocum spotted Cha'to again, the flat-nosed wolf had closed in on one of the archers that had crept just a bit too close to the rest of the hunters. An arrow was lodged in the wolf's side, which did nothing to keep it from clamping its jaws around the Apache's hip and bringing the man down with a few powerful twists of its head. To his credit, the archer didn't panic even as his own blood spilled onto the desert floor. Instead, he grabbed the arrow he'd been trying to notch and jabbed it repeatedly into Cha'to's side. That only stoked the wolf's fire as he buried his snout beneath the Apache's chin.

It was tough for Slocum to watch as the Indian's throat was ripped out, but he kept his eye on his target while gazing along the top of the Winchester. He fired a shot that knocked the big wolf off its balance and another that sent it rolling onto its side. Cha'to yelped in pain as the arrows embedded in its body were jammed in even deeper between the earth and its own weight.

A sharp cry from Snake Catcher drew Slocum's attention toward the Apache leader and two of his warriors. The black wolf was still on its feet and ran at Snake Catcher without an ounce of fear to slow its progress. "Damn it," Slocum growled as he levered in a fresh round. That action was necessary, but wasted the precious time needed to fire a shot to keep Snake Catcher from being mauled. The black wolf's paws thumped against the Apache's chest, knocking him over with ease. Two of the other warriors closed in, but were about two steps too far away to get to their leader in time. A shot cracked through the air, clipping the wolf's ear and snapping its attention to the man who'd fired it.

Jack sat in his saddle, still holding his smoking pistol and gaping slack-jawed at the black wolf he'd just angered.

When the wolf began charging at him, he looked ready to throw his gun at it and ride for the hills. Not necessarily the closest hills. Any hills.

The wolf's coat was bloodied, but its wounds only made it move faster as it bolted toward its attacker. Even though Slocum knew he could fire a quick shot, he doubted he could hit the erratically moving canine. The wolf wouldn't even take notice of a shot that didn't bring it down, so Slocum avoided wasting any ammunition and rode to a better spot. Jack snapped his reins and got his horse moving fast enough to keep from catching the brunt of the wolf's attack. The beast's claws scraped against the horse's hind-quarter and its teeth ripped into its flesh, causing the black gelding to buck and lash out with its rear legs. One hoof came within an inch of the wolf's temple, but the other hit it squarely in the chest to knock it back.

Slocum brought his Winchester to his shoulder and took his time aiming. Although he wasn't delaying just to watch Jack squirm, he had to admit that was an amusing bonus. He pulled his trigger and shot the wolf through the center of its body. The impact sent it skidding as a pair of arrows sailed in to scrape against the ground where it had been. When the wolf came to a stop, it scrambled to its feet and started to snarl before one more arrow dug into its neck.

Looking back for the source of the volley, Slocum found Flying Spear and one of his archers hastily notching another set of arrows. They kept their bows, backs, and shoulders steady so as not to lose their trajectory while reloading. Their arms moved swiftly to notch their arrows, draw them back, and send them through the air before reaching back for another one.

The arrows whistled toward their mark. Most of them thumped solidly into the wolf's flesh, and only one from each archer snapped against the ground. Although it seemed like overkill, Slocum lined up a shot and sent a bullet through the black wolf's head.

Only one animal remained and it wasn't inclined to run. Finding it was easy, since Snake Catcher and three of his warriors had moved in to surround it. Cha'to barked, snarled, and snapped angrily at the Apache. When one of the warriors took half a step toward the wolf, another came in from the opposite side, but Cha'to didn't take the bait. The wolf barely flinched toward the first warrior and reared up to twist its arrow-studded body around toward the second.

Because he didn't have a clear shot, Slocum rode toward the party. He could only watch as the Apache warrior was knocked down and brutally mauled. The Indian screamed as the wolf's snarls took on a wet, muffled quality. The rest of the warriors closed in until Slocum could see nothing more than a mass of struggling bodies.

He arrived and swung down from his saddle, tossing the Winchester so he could hastily draw his Schofield. Another Apache was tossed aside, but scrambled to get back to his feet to join the fray. Slocum waded in to find Snake Catcher clinging to the wolf's back with both arms wrapped around its neck. At first, it looked as if the Apache leader was struggling to hang on. Then Slocum saw the purpose in his movements as well as the short, curved knife in Snake Catcher's right hand.

Snake Catcher's face was twisted into a vicious mask as he drove the little blade into Cha'to again and again. The wolf continued to struggle, but was distracted by other Apache hunters, who continued to poke and jab at him with spears and knives. Finally, the wolf let out a piercing cry as one of Snake Catcher's blows dug in deeper than the rest. Snake Catcher's blade was completely embedded within the beast, so he gripped the handle tightly and dragged it up toward the animal's throat.

It was a lethal display of courage and tenacity that Slocum had rarely seen before. No matter how much devastation had been inflicted upon him or his men, Snake Catcher attacked the wolf from point-blank range. In its final moments, the animal seemed vaguely confused that it was unable to bring the Apache down. Even after the short blade opened the wolf's jugular, the beast continued to fight.

Slocum stood nearby with his pistol at the ready. "Get away from it," he said. "I'll finish it off."

But Snake Catcher hung on until the last bit of fight left Cha'to's body. The rage that had been on his face slowly melted into grim satisfaction. "No," he said while shoving the carcass away. His own warriors knew better than to help him to his feet despite the many cuts and gouges on his limbs and torso. Once he was standing, Snake Catcher gazed down at the wolf as its struggles dwindled down to a twitching back leg. "Let him die in his own time. He has fought well enough to earn that much."

"To hell with that!" Jack shouted as he tumbled from his saddle in a sloppy dismount. "Just make sure he don't get away!"

"He's not going anywhere," Slocum said.

Stepping up close so he could speak to Slocum alone, Jack snarled loud enough for the others to hear him anyway. "Then let's look for a den around here."

Slocum looked over at Snake Catcher and received a nod. When the two white men mounted their horses and rode away, none of the Apache moved to stop them.

14

Slocum couldn't decide if Jack had a knack for sniffing out wolf dens or if he was just somehow connected to the beast that had made off with his fingers, but they did find a promising hole at the base of some rocks gathered around the base of an old tree. There was barely enough space for an animal the size of Cha'to to get in, which meant Jack had to wriggle around inside with half his legs hanging outside. When he shouted for Slocum to pull him out, his hand was coated in scat and his face had acquired a fresh layer of scrapes.

"Nothin'," Jack sighed. "But it looked like those things weren't in there for very long."

"Have you done a lot of hunting?"

"Not really. Just common sense." Holding up his rancid left hand, he explained, "There wasn't enough in there for me to think that—"

Slocum stopped him and walked back to his horse. "Don't need to hear the whole story. If you're done here, so am I."

"I am. Now we gotta track them Apache back to their real camp. Think you're up to that?"

Slocum had already found a spot on the horizon and nodded in that direction so Jack could see the pair of lean silhouettes watching them from afar. He couldn't be certain who it was, but he would have placed a good-sized bet that one of those figures was Flying Spear. "I don't think we'll have to do any more tracking today."

Since his eyes had become accustomed to the shadows within the wolf's den, it took Jack an extra couple of seconds to spot them. When he did, he mumbled to himself and climbed onto his horse's back.

As he rode toward the ridge, Slocum waved at the figures to let them know he'd spotted them. To his surprise, one of the figures waved back.

"I don't like this," Jack said.

"What would you prefer? A few arrows flying in our direction?"

"No, but them Injuns only wanted some extra firepower along for that hunt. What the hell could they want now?"

"One good way to find out," Slocum said.

"I'd rather track them on our own."

"Right. Great idea. They're already watching us now, so we'll just mosey some other way until they lose interest. Then, we'll track them back to their camp, sneak in, and help ourselves to their prize catch."

Jack winced, but tried to play it off. "It's a thought."

"You ever try to sneak up on an Apache?"

"No."

"You'd have better luck holding your hand in front of that wolf's mouth and asking politely for it to cough up your fingers."

"No need to be crude," Jack scowled.

Slocum snapped his reins and chuckled, "That's a hell of a thing coming from a man with wolf dung under his fingernails."

Jack didn't even try to defend himself. Instead, he wiped his hand across the front of his shirt and urged his gelding to catch up to Slocum's stallion.

Less than two minutes into their ride, the figures disappeared from the ridge and showed up again at a spot on lower ground, waiting idly as if they had been there all day long. Flying Spear and one of the other archers still wore the blood on their faces that had been put there during their fight with Cha'to. Before Slocum could close the gap between them, the Apache turned to the southwest and tapped their knees against their animals' sides.

"Mind telling us where we're headed?" Slocum asked.

Without turning around to look at them, Flying Spear shouted, "Back to our camp. Snake Catcher wants to speak to our chief to tell him about how well you fought." Casting half a glance over his shoulder, he added, "How well *one* of you fought."

Although Jack kept grousing as he always did, Slocum took some comfort from the fact that he hadn't spotted any other Apache keeping watch from a position that lent itself to an ambush. Also, Flying Spear actually rode with his back to them in a show of implicit trust. Add those things to what had already been said outright and Slocum figured he and Jack had earned the Apache's favor. If they hadn't gotten it after battling Cha'to and his pack, Slocum didn't know what the hell it would take.

They rode along a trail that skirted around the spot where they'd killed the wolves earlier that morning. Despite the fact that Slocum had covered so much ground, fired so many rounds, and come face to face with beasts that could very well have been spit up from the devil's belly, it was still early in the day. Sometimes, there was so much living and dying packed into such a short amount of time that it was easy to lose track of how much had actually passed. Even the Apache rode with their backs straight and their heads held high as if they'd fully rested in the brief respite.

The trail led up into the Potrillos, but only high enough for Slocum to get a good look down at the desert floor. The terrain was manageable and their horses traversed it well enough. That is, until Jack's gelding nearly lost its footing and almost dumped him off the side of a steep slope. He hung on with his one good hand, gritted his teeth, and clenched every muscle at his disposal until the horse leveled off and continued plodding after the rest of the group. When Slocum offered to help, he was waved off angrily. Wasn't the first time. Probably wouldn't be the last.

The Apache settlement was in a shallow basin along the western edge of the mountain range, surrounded by trees that were higher than the closest rocks. Before he caught sight of the first hint of a camp, Slocum could smell the cooking fires. His stomach reminded him of how long it had been since he'd had a decent meal by snarling louder than the wolves he'd been hunting. Not only was there meat being cooked, but he could also smell something that could have been bread or some sort of wheat cakes.

From a distance, the tops of the Apache teepees blended in almost completely with the trees surrounding them. If he hadn't known what he was looking for, Slocum might have passed them by. At the moment, however, there was no way he could have missed the settlement. Smoke rose from the fires, and many voices were raised in celebration. By the time Flying Spear led them into the trees, some of the voices blended together into a spirited song.

"Looks like they knew we was comin'!" Jack shouted over the gleeful noise.

Slocum turned to look at the other man to see if he was kidding. He couldn't tell if the smile on Jack's face was proof of that or not, so he let it rest. "Just don't say anything stupid to ruin the party, okay?"

"Why would I do something like that?"

"And don't mention what you're after. Just give us a bit of time to see where we stand."

"You still don't trust them all the way?"

Slocum chewed on that for a moment while watching Flying Spear and the other archer return greetings from the first among the tribe to spot the arriving horses. His knee-jerk response would have been that he trusted these men as much as he would any others who'd fought and bled alongside him. He'd dealt with Indians from other tribes, and this wasn't the first time he'd crossed paths with the Apache. Perhaps it was that previous experience, more than anything else, that made Slocum stop to think before answering.

There were many tribes and they all had a wide assortment of people in them, just like any other society. There were plenty of things that set them apart from the rest, but they were still folks trying to find their way like any others no matter what color their skin happened to be. The Apache were different. They separated themselves from other tribes just as much as they separated from the white men. Their tactics in war were renowned for their efficiency and brutality. When they weren't charging across a battlefield, they were even deadlier. Some federal troops only guessed that an Apache raiding party had taken out the rest of their men because of what was left behind. When Apache wanted to kill without being seen, they might as well have been ghosts.

In the end, it was his knowledge of their ruthlessness that gave Slocum the most comfort. If these Apache had wanted him or Jack dead, they would have already made their move. Having superior numbers as well as the benefit of familiar terrain at their disposal, there was no need for them to lie. From what he'd seen of Snake Catcher and Flying Spear, Slocum doubted those two would lower themselves to the level of stringing along an inferior enemy.

"Just sit tight and keep your eyes open," Slocum told the man riding beside him. "Let's see if we can get some of whatever they're cooking."

"Amen to that!" Jack proclaimed.

The camp was larger than Slocum had anticipated. Laid

out in a simple horseshoe formation, a semicircle of teepees had been erected on the perimeter with a few smaller tents pitched throughout a space that was roughly the size of a small town square. A fire blazed toward the back of the settlement, and a corral was roped off toward the front. Flying Spear led them to the corral and climbed down from his horse's back with ease. The other archer motioned for Slocum and Jack to follow suit and even helped tie their reins off beside a wooden frame with tanned hides stretched inside to form a low water trough.

Where the hunters' camp had seemed quiet and desolate, this one was teeming with life. Indians wearing long, flowing buckskins smiled with deeply wrinkled faces framed in silver hair. Children ran up to catch a glimpse of the newest arrivals while others scampered around on all fours to reenact tales that had already been spread about the early morning hunt. When Slocum looked down at one round-faced little boy, the kid squatted down, stared up at him, and howled.

"They say you are the great hunters who stood with Snake Catcher to bring the mighty Cha'to to his knees," Flying Spear explained.

Jack did his best to maintain his dignity while flopping from his saddle using his awkward one-handed technique. "Well, ain't they right?"

"Children believe in many ridiculous things," the archer replied. "That does not make them right."

Slocum swatted Jack's shoulder good-naturedly. "He's got you there."

"I shot some of them wolves, too, you know."

"I know. Tell it to them!"

Without hesitating, Jack hunkered down and locked eyes with the feral little boy. Baring his teeth, he snarled and then lifted his chin to howl up at an imaginary moon. The little boy was all too happy to join him.

Flying Spear watched Jack awhile before shaking his

head and moving along. Slocum was all too happy to join him.

"Any chance we can get something to eat?" Slocum asked.

"Of course," Flying Spear replied. "The feast is being prepared in your honor." He stopped and turned in a few crisp movements. Lifting his chin just a bit more, he said, "You fought bravely, John Slocum."

"Just John is fine."

"You fought bravely, John. Much braver than I was expecting."

"And what were you expecting?"

"I thought I would have the pleasure of watching you run away out of fear or try to escape before fulfilling your vow to fight. Then, I would have gladly put an arrow in your back."

"Sorry to disappoint you."

"I am not sorry." Reaching out to place a hand upon Slocum's shoulder, he added, "I am honored to fight with you and proud to share the feast that is being prepared."

"The pleasure's all mine," Slocum said earnestly. "And I'd like to apologize on behalf of my friend over there."

When Flying Spear glanced over, he found Jack snarling and yapping while the little boy went through the motions of shooting him with arrows. "He did better than I thought he would during the hunt. I also expected to shoot him while he was running away."

"I was expecting you to shoot him, too," Slocum said with a shrug. "Guess we don't always get what we want."

Flying Spear broke into a wide grin. He looked over to Jack, started laughing, and then walked to the group of hunters gathering by the fire.

Jack saw the laughing Indian and climbed to his feet. He was in good spirits until the boy tried to pull him back down again by tugging anxiously on his bandaged right hand. Although Jack winced and pulled his arm away from the child's eager grasp, he kept his good nature intact as he patted the boy's head with his left hand. As he walked over to Slocum, he said, "Didn't think an Injun could smile like that."

"Actually," Slocum replied, "neither did I. You did a good job during the hunt, Jack. Better than anyone was expecting."

"Is that what you two were talking about?"

"More or less."

"That's what I thought. My ears were burnin'. I knew that one there liked me, though," Jack added as he nodded toward Flying Spear. "I could tell by the way he was always watching what I did. Like he was just waiting for me to do something great."

Now Slocum was chuckling as he shook his head and let the other man dream. "Come on. Let's get some of that food before it's all gone."

Walking across the camp was more of an ordeal than Slocum had anticipated. Although there wasn't a lot of ground to cover, they were distracted nearly every step of the way by wide, beaming faces eager to either congratulate them or ask for a retelling of what had happened. Most of those faces belonged to children, but there were a few young ladies who also approached Slocum and Jack. The Apache women weren't as boisterous, but Jack's willingness to stop and brag impeded their progress across the camp more than an army of enthusiastic youngsters. Finally, Slocum left him behind so he could make his way to a spot where a woman sat in front of a flat clay pot that was being warmed over a shallow bed of coals.

She wore a simple tunic that was long enough to cover the legs she kept tucked beneath her while tending to whatever was simmering. Long, straight black hair flowed down her back and was held in place by several leather cords adorned with beads. Full cheeks and lips made her one of the prettiest sights in the entire camp, and she became even prettier when she smiled at Slocum.

"Hello, miss," he said. "Don't know if you understand what I'm saying, but—"

"I understand," she told him.

"Good. And you speak English pretty well, too."

"You know that from two words? Very impressive."

"You got me," Slocum chuckled as he sat down across the coals from her. "But you do speak very well. Better than my friend anyway."

She looked over to where Jack was still talking with an Apache woman with generous hips and breasts who seemed to find everything he said hilarious and fascinating. "Imala must like the way he speaks."

"Yeah, but who knows what lies he's telling her. My name's John."

Although her smile faded a bit, it was more out of quiet reservation than displeasure. She averted her eyes momentarily, but when she pointed them at Slocum again, he could see they were as brilliant as two finely polished pieces of amber. "I am Nitika."

"That's a pretty name."

She looked down at the shallow pot she was tending, reached inside, and removed a flat piece of bread that resembled a cross between a griddle cake and a tortilla. "I made this for you." A bit of color flushed into her dark cheeks as she quickly added, "For all of the returning hunters."

Slocum took the bread and sampled it. Although clearly made from oats and some other grains, there was a sweetness just beneath the surface that tasted better the longer he savored it. "Hope you made a lot because that's awfully good."

"There is also meat being cooked there," she said while motioning toward one of the smaller tents. "Or I could get some for you."

As much as Slocum wanted both of them to stay where

they were, he noticed several members of the hunting party walking to and from the makeshift smokehouse with large portions of what smelled like venison in their hands. When Jack caught the scent, he looked at the cooking fires like a dog with its ears pricked up.

"Maybe I should hurry up and get some of that meat myself," Slocum said, honestly thinking that Nitika might not be able to move fast enough. "Just so long as you promise to be here when I get back."

"Just go. There is much more for you to do than talk to me."

Slocum was certain she was right, but he couldn't think of anything that appealed to him more at that moment.

15

The feast was an unending stream of breads, meats, and cakes. Slocum had barely gotten ahold of some venison before Jack came along to tear off a chunk for himself. Until Snake Catcher appeared behind them, Slocum had lost sight of the hunting party's leader.

"Come," Snake Catcher said while walking inside. "Our chief wants to speak with us about the hunt."

"Can't we eat first?" Jack groaned.

Before any of the Apache could voice the disdain that appeared on their faces, Slocum dropped a heavy hand onto Jack's shoulder and shoved him away from the meat. "If you're in such a hurry, I'm sure you can take what you can carry, get on your horse, and ride away."

"Fine," Jack said while stuffing venison into his mouth like a squirrel filling his cheeks with acorns. "But there better be some of this left when we're through."

Slocum continued shoving the other man all the way into the tent where Snake Catcher waited like a grim sentry.

The interior walls were decorated by paintings and scorched black in the middle by all the fires that had been stoked there throughout the years. There was a fire going now, which was just large enough for the flames to be seen above a ring of stones and a wooden frame that held a small pot high enough to cook its contents without burning the wood. Fragrant smoke curled up from the pot, giving the air a vaguely dreamlike quality.

Inside, Flying Spear and three men from the hunting party sat talking in subdued tones to tribal elders with long, silver manes of coarse hair. The oldest kept his clouded eyes fixed upon the brewing pot while nodding as if to a faraway song that only he could hear.

"Sit there," Snake Catcher said while motioning to an open space on the ground between Flying Spear and one of the other Apache who'd taken a large role in bringing down the pack of wolves using nothing but a tomahawk.

Jack held up a dainty finger and said, "I got a question."

Tightening his grip on Jack's shoulder, Slocum pulled him close enough to fiercely whisper, "I swear to all that's holy if you ask about food, I'll stuff your head into that fire."

After looking down at the fire, over to Slocum, and back to the fire again, Jack shifted his eyes toward Snake Catcher. "Forgot what I was gonna say."

Slocum patted Jack's back with enough force to make him stagger the few steps required to get him to where they were supposed to sit down. Although the conversation didn't stop with their arrival, the rest of the men gathered in the tent did take a moment to size up Slocum and Jack with lingering glares. Even the members of the hunting party stared them down as if seeing the white men for the first time.

Motioning toward the old man with the faraway look in his eyes, Snake Catcher said, "This is our chief. Gopan."

"Pleased to meet ya," Jack said as he tried to stretch his body up enough to reach out and shake the chief's hand.

Slocum pushed him back down again while easing himself into a seated position and placed his hands upon his knees. When Jack turned to look at him, he took note of how Slocum was sitting and had enough sense to mimic it. "I'm John Slocum and this is my partner, Jack Halsey."

As annoyed as Jack had been a moment ago, his countenance became much more agreeable when he was referred to as a partner. Appeased for the moment, he sat quietly and let Slocum do the talking.

Gopan's voice rumbled like a tremor emanating from the ground beneath the camp. His lips barely moved, and his eyes never strayed from the fire as he spoke in his own language. The man beside him looked older than the trees ringing the campsite, but still younger than the Apache chief. "He asks why you men joined the hunt for Cha'to."

"We were already tracking the wolves when your hunters found us," Slocum explained.

"The wolves hurt your people?"

Since the chief hadn't spoken, Slocum assumed the question came from the younger of the two elders. "The one you call Cha'to attacked my friend."

Not needing any more incentive than that, Jack held out his right hand and tore at the bandages. When he finally pulled away enough of the bloody dressing to reveal his ravaged fingers, he displayed them proudly and declared, "That animal ripped the hell outta me! I hired John here to help make myself whole again!"

So much for respectful silence.

Although the Apache took time to examine Jack's hand, none of them seemed overly impressed by the damage that had been done. The man sitting beside the chief leaned over to speak to the eldest Apache while motioning toward Jack. Gopan didn't show much of a reaction, which wasn't a surprise considering his face looked as if it had been carved from a petrified tree trunk.

Flying Spear leaned over to Slocum and said, "The man beside Gopan is Ilesh. He is what you would call our shaman. He is not from our tribe, but he is a great help to us."

"What's he saying?"

"He tells your words to our chief. Gopan knows much of the white man's tongue, but prefers to listen to the words of our people."

Snake Catcher had taken the other seat next to Gopan. When the chief turned toward him and motioned for the hunter to get closer, Snake Catcher did so with great reverence.

"Now Gopan wants to hear the story from one who lived through it," Flying Spear explained.

"Will you get a chance to say your piece?" Slocum asked.

"We all will. By the end of the night, you will grow tired of hearing about it."

"Not all of us will," Slocum said while nodding over to Jack.

Although Jack was obviously perturbed by being the butt of so many jokes, he was too nervous to speak up about it. Slocum had thought about easing up on the poor fellow, but saw how much the Apache archer enjoyed hearing those jokes. Sometimes, a man had to take a few short knocks to avoid the killing blows. And since that man wasn't him, Slocum felt even better about it.

After Snake Catcher was through, the chief looked at the rest of the men while opening his arms as if he meant to embrace them. Beads and feathers hung from his sleeves and rattled in his hair whenever he turned his head. As he spoke in his rasping monotone, his head continued to bob up and down.

Flying Spear leaned over again and said, "He asks to hear the story told by all of you."

"Yeah, I caught that much."

The archer looked at Slocum with newfound respect. "You understand our tongue?"

"Bits and pieces. I picked up a few words here and there." In truth, most of what Slocum had acquired as far as Indian languages came from having to know when a raiding party meant to kill him or not. Since relations with this tribe seemed to be coming along so nicely, he decided to keep that part to himself.

Without needing to be asked, Flying Spear went first. Although he relayed his account purely in his native language, his expression remained stoic and his hands stayed upon his folded legs. Slocum could understand enough to recognize a bare-bones retelling of the hunt. The tales picked up a bit once the other members of the hunting party lent their voices to the mix. They waited for Jack to speak next, who looked over at Slocum.

"What are they lookin' at?" Jack asked.

"They're telling about the hunt," Slocum reminded him. "Now it's your turn."

"What should I say?"

"You were more than ready to brag to that lady outside. Now's your chance to impress the rest of us."

Although Jack brightened up at that prospect, he sobered quickly when he saw the stern expressions worn by the tribal elders. Gopan especially took the wind from his sails as he stared expectantly at him with his clouded eyes. "All I did was try to shoot the damn things when I got the chance," Jack muttered.

"You shot one?" Ilesh asked.

"That's right. One of them rushed me."

"Which one?"

"The black one, I think."

Half of the elders nodded approvingly, and the others followed suit once Jack's words were translated for them. Seeing that was enough to lift Jack's spirits again. "That was a mean one, all right. But not as mean as that flat-nosed son of a bitch."

"You . . . faced Cha'to?" Gopan asked.

Hearing him speak English seemed to surprise the rest of the Apache as much as the two white men. Jack maintained his composure well enough to nod and say, "Yes, sir. I did."

"Tell us."

"I was in my camp. It was outside of a town called Rocas Rojas. Do any of you know where that is? Maybe you call it by some Injun name."

"We know it," Ilesh snapped.

"All right. Well, I was in my camp and this wolf ran up and attacked me. Chatto," Jack said, slaughtering the pronunciation. "That's what you call him. I think that name must mean devil or demon in some language because that's what it was."

Although many of the elders bristled at the loose translation that had nothing at all to do with their language, none of them bothered to correct him.

"It ran up like it was spat from the bowels of hell!" Jack proclaimed. "Charged at me, ran me down, and tore me up no matter how hard I fought back."

"You fought back?" Ilesh asked.

"Well . . . like I said . . . it took me by surprise. What matters is what it done to me. Look for yerself! I ain't whole no more. That's why I had to come after that thing."

Slocum had to give Jack credit. Even though he'd already admitted his story about needing to find the piece of himself that was lost was absolute bullshit, he stuck to it like it was gospel. When he got nothing but a bunch of blank stares from the Apache, Jack even had the gall to look surprised.

"You were wounded," Ilesh said. "Like many of our men were wounded."

"But . . . that wolf took away part of me."

"And Cha'to took the lives of women and children. Do you expect to find their spirits in the bellies of those animals?"

"Not as such."

"Then do not try to make the blood you spilled seem more important than what was spilled by others," Ilesh scolded. "Tell us why you needed to hunt Cha'to. I look upon you and don't see the same kind of man as when I look at that one. John Slocum walks like a hunter and speaks like a hunter."

"But he ain't even had his turn to speak yet!" Jack groused.

Slocum thought about telling Jack to quit before burying himself any deeper, but knew it wouldn't do a lick of good.

"I have watched him, and Snake Catcher has told me of his deeds," Ilesh continued. "Even now I can see he is closer to our warriors than you could ever hope to be."

Jack seemed genuinely offended by that. "But—"

"And do not try to tell me of how you must make yourself whole again. You have been speaking about rituals that mean no more to you than does the smoke rising from this fire."

Jack looked at the fire and then to the smoke as if he actually needed to see the black wisps in order to comprehend what he was being told.

"So," Ilesh said with a sober finality, "why would a man like you make it your business to pursue Cha'to?"

"I'm a hunter."

Gopan's eyes narrowed with suspicion, and half of his wizened mouth curled into a grin to match.

"All right," Jack said. "I'm after something else."

Snake Catcher looked at Ilesh while Flying Spear looked at Slocum. When he saw the archer's questioning glance, Slocum merely shrugged his shoulders. He could have spoken up about the ring, but none of the elders seemed interested. Also, it was somewhat refreshing to see Jack get raked over the coals for all of his double-talking flimflam.

"What are you after?" Ilesh asked.

"That wolf took my fingers. Do you doubt that much?"

Ilesh and the chief looked at Snake Catcher. The leader of the hunting party nodded. "I believe that."

Looking back at Jack, Ilesh said, "Then so do I."

Jack sat up straight as if to accept high praise instead of the minor concession he'd been given. "When those wolves attacked me, I was wearing a ring. Ask him," he said while waving toward Slocum. "He'll tell you!"

Every Apache eye turned toward Slocum, making him feel as if he'd been tossed into the pot that was cooking slowly over the fire in the middle of the room. "That's what he told me," he said.

Again, Jack reacted as if he'd gotten a reprieve from on high. "There you go! You trust him, so you can trust me."

"I trust that you told this same story to John Slocum," Ilesh said. "I tell many stories to our children. That does not make them all true."

Jack began to squirm. That happened to most weasels when getting called out on something, but lying about a rite to the people who should have held that rite as sacred was a whole different animal. When the ones he had to answer to were old men who looked as if they'd weathered more storms than Jack had ever known, *squirming* wasn't quite strong enough of a word.

"That wolf took something from me other than my fingers," Jack said. "I'll swear on a stack of Bibles to that effect . . . or whatever you Injuns want me to swear on."

"Good lord," Slocum sighed.

Jack's ignorant talk barely made a dent in the Apache chief or his shaman. Gopan drew a breath, reached for a pouch on his belt, and handed it to Ilesh. The younger of the two elders opened the pouch and dropped something into his hand. "You say you are missing a ring?" Ilesh asked.

"Yes, sir."

"And you will swear on your life to this?"

When Jack paused, Slocum whispered, "Just swear to it, for Christ's sake."

Jack's mouth tightened into a grim line and his eyes fixed upon Ilesh's hand. Finally, he said, "Swearing on my life . . . may be a little drastic."

"Drastic?"

"Yeah. It means harsh or—"

"I know the word, white man!" Ilesh bellowed in a voice that filled the teepee and caused even the strongest among the hunting party to recoil. "What about *disgraceful*? Do you know this word?"

"Yeah."

"I know this word because your people have thrown it at mine for many years. You call us *savages* and *disgraceful* for raiding your towns and killing in retribution for all that has been done to us. I know what this word means, and now I want to make sure you know what I think of a sniveling little coward who tells lies to the same men who fought and bled against the wolves that would have killed you without a thought."

"Look, I . . ." But Jack didn't have to be scolded for his mouth to be shut. All he needed was to see the chief's clouded eyes boring through him like sunlight focused through a magnifying glass.

"Three of our hunters were killed," Ilesh continued. "Three more are resting now after spilling their blood while you sit here healthy enough to speak to our chief. Tell me why you hunted Cha'to or you disgrace our people by disgracing yourself in front of them."

Jack took a breath and shot half a glance over at Slocum. He didn't seem to have it in him to do much more than that before saying, "That wolf took my fingers. When he did, I wasn't wearing no ring."

"Damn it," Slocum growled.

"I came after that wolf because I was holding something when I was attacked. I hid it in my camp, heard the wolves, and dug it up so I could get the hell away from there. The wolves got to me quicker than I thought they would. I was still holding it, and when they came at me, they took it with my fingers."

Ignoring everyone else in the area, Slocum faced Jack and asked, "What was it? What the hell was it that caused this much grief?"

Although Jack's words had come out of him like water from a cracked bucket, he was squirming too hard to say much of anything anymore. Slocum lunged, grabbed the front of his shirt, and stood up while dragging him along with him. "Tell me, God damn it!" he said while drawing his Schofield and jamming its barrel underneath Jack's chin. "Or by God, I'll give these men a treat by blasting your head clean off'a your neck!"

"It was a key!" Jack said.

"A key?"

"That's right! I swear it!"

"Why the hell should I believe you?"

"Because," Ilesh said, "I also believe him. It was a key." Extending his hand so Slocum could see what he'd taken from the pouch, he opened his fist to reveal a small key that glistened in the firelight. "I also believe this is the key."

16

That was the key all right. Slocum could tell as much by the look on Jack's face. Like any liar, he was relieved to finally have the truth brought to light. It was a difference that was so drastic, Slocum felt like a fool for not having pieced it all together before. He threw Jack aside as if he were tossing garbage from a moving train and stormed out of the teepee. Rather than walk among the rest of the tribe that was still preparing the feast, he circled around the back of the teepee and walked until there was nothing but open ground and trees in front of him.

Slocum patted his shirt pocket and found half of a cigar that had been stuck in there since the last poker game he'd played just over a week ago. It was burnt and stale, but tasted good enough to distract him for a few moments until his heart stopped hammering within his chest. His pulse quickened again when he heard footsteps coming around the teepee.

"If that's you, Jack, do yourself a favor and walk somewhere else."

The other person didn't say a word, which was enough

to tell Slocum that it wasn't Jack. When he looked over, Slocum was surprised to find a face that looked as if it had been fashioned from weathered driftwood.

"You should not treat your friend so harshly," Gopan said.

Shocked to be in the presence of the Apache chief, Slocum forgot about the cigar in his mouth until the smoke stung the back of his nose. When he removed it, he didn't know whether he should stamp it out or apologize for not having one to offer the old man. He settled for keeping the cigar in his hand as he said, "That one's hardly a friend of mine."

"Then you walk many miles through much fire to protect a stranger."

Gopan's voice was barely more than a grating wheeze and yet it carried more weight than most men's loudest boasts. Hearing it, Slocum couldn't help calming himself so he could behave properly in the chief's presence. "He fed me a lot of bullshit," Slocum said with a wince afterward. "Pardon my language."

"I have heard much worse," Gopan chuckled. "Your friend is a liar."

"Yep. And I'm a fool for riding with him this far."

"No," Gopan said while gazing out at the trees surrounding his tribe. "He is a liar. Just as Cha'to was a strong, hungry animal. We had to hunt Cha'to, but it is not our place to condemn him."

"He was just doing his job," Slocum said.

Gopan clasped his hands in front of him and laughed as the faraway look once more drifted into his eyes. At that moment, he just seemed like a gentle old man taking in the sights. "Yes. Just doing his job. I like that."

"If you don't mind me saying, you're not like most of the other Indian chiefs I have seen."

"I am just a man. Older than most. My tribe is made of people. They want me to lead them. I do."

"I'm sorry about Jack."

"Snake Catcher told me about the hunt. I listened to the stories that were told around my fire. I heard enough to know that Jack Halsey did his part to make the hunt a victory. Some of my own warriors rode after Cha'to in righteous anger over losing their loved ones to the teeth of those wolves. Some rode for motives that were not so noble. In the end, Cha'to will kill no more. That is what matters most."

Slocum nodded and took a puff from his cigar. The stale taste was growing on him, and since the chief didn't seem to mind the smoke, he refrained from stamping it out. "So . . . about that key."

Gopan smiled and stood like a totem that had been planted deep enough to withstand an earthquake. "Ilesh brought it to me."

"How did he get it?"

"I do not know. Does it matter?"

"Yeah. It does to me. There's been too many things getting past me and I've been too content to let them slide."

"Why would you help a man you dislike so much?" Gopan asked.

"I took the job because I knew Jack had the money to pay the fee he offered. I also knew Jack was full of shit . . ." Slocum paused and felt a pang of conscience when he cursed in front of the chief. He was no stranger to harsh language, but speaking that way to Gopan just didn't set well with him. "Knew that, but didn't think he was into anything terrible. Also, there are men after him. They came at us in Rocas Rojas and we were lucky to get away."

"Of course there are."

"Do you know about them, too?" Slocum asked.

"No, but men who lie frequently have to run from those they have angered."

"Yeah, well, the men coming after Jack are a bit more than angry. I was gonna head out to see if they've tracked us this far."

"What will you do when you find these men?"

"I don't know. Maybe hand Jack over to them. The little bastard's got it coming."

"You don't think that," Gopan said with absolute certainty.

"I don't?"

"Maybe he has it coming, but you don't think about handing him over to be slaughtered. You are not that kind of man."

"Maybe you don't know me very well," Slocum said.

"I have gotten to be this old by being able to see who men are as soon as they reveal themselves. You may be surprised with how little time you have to wait for them to do this. John Slocum is not the sort of man to hand another over to be killed. Not unless he is a much worse man than the weasel who rode with him against Cha'to."

Slocum had been the cause of many deaths, but the chief was right. He wasn't about to end a man's life just for being a pain in the ass. "I should still go and see if those other fellows are coming after him. If not for Jack's sake, for the sake of your tribe."

"Our scouts always protect us. My tribe has many enemies. We have withstood the guns of the white man's army. We can withstand a few bandits chasing a weasel."

"I saw these men before. I'll be able to pick them out as something other than a couple of men riding through the Potrillos."

"Then go with my scouts, but fill your belly first. The feast, after all, is for all of those who killed Cha'to."

"Don't mind if I do." Slocum wanted to shake the chief's hand, but the old man kept his hands clasped firmly in place across the front of his body as he turned to walk back around the largest teepee. After he was gone, Slocum stood and finished his cigar. Another set of footsteps found him, but he knew his luck wasn't good enough to dodge the same bullet twice.

"John? Mind if I have a word?"

"Figured it was you, Jack. What do you want?"

Jack approached tentatively and made certain to stop just outside Slocum's reach. "Like I said. Just a word."

The cigar flared in Slocum's mouth. He chewed on the smoke and then expelled it in a strong breath.

"Didn't mean to lie to you, John."

"Really? So it just slipped?"

"I suppose I just—"

Slocum wheeled around to stare directly into Jack's eyes. His jaw clamped shut almost tightly enough to drive his teeth clean through his cigar when he said, "You don't owe me an explanation. I knew what kind of asshole you were the moment I heard you scream like a little girl as you staggered into that doctor's office."

"Hey now!" Jack said. "In my defense, I just lost most of my hand!"

"Spare me. I've heard men that had been gut-shot whine less than you. But fine. I'll give you that one. Then it turns out you've got killers coming after you. To be honest, that was never much of a surprise."

"Yeah, I heard you and the chief talking about that."

"I was the one who took the job you offered," Slocum said. "I've worked for plenty of assholes and I'll work for plenty more. You owe me money, so hand it over."

Jack's hands reflexively went for his belt, telling Slocum precisely where the cash was being stored at the moment. "Those men are still after me. They could still find me."

"But you got what you were after with that wolf pack. I want the rest of what you owe me to pay for the portion of the job that's been done."

"And what about the rest of the job?" Jack asked.

"Take your pick," Slocum said from behind the stump of a cigar clenched in his mouth. "You can either consider my payment a show of good faith for putting up with your moaning for this long, or you can consider it a quick way to keep me from putting a bullet through your head just to rid myself of you."

Jack's smile was wide, but shaky. "I heard you talking to the chief, remember? You said you wouldn't wanna shoot me."

"I believe *he* said something along those lines. Not me."

"Well, he also said you're not the sort of man to just hand someone like me over to die. Killing me is even worse, ain't it?"

"Funny, but it seemed so when I was talking to the chief. Now I'm not so sure."

Jack's smile had been wavering at first, but now that he was being pushed a little further, he was unable to keep it in place. Letting it go along with the breath that had been in his lungs, he reached beneath his shirt and pulled out some cash. "Fine," he said while handing it over. "Take it. I don't know if that's all of it, but there you go."

Slocum took the money and arranged the bills so they could be folded and tucked into his pocket. After studying Jack's face for all of two seconds, he said, "You didn't think I was going to take it, did you?"

"Not really. The offer was more of a show of good faith," Jack replied, putting the emphasis on *show*.

Slocum said, "Tell me about the key."

Jack eyed the money for as long as he could before admitting to himself that he wasn't getting it back. "It unlocks a strongbox that's buried in . . ." His eyes flicked to Slocum's before snapping away again. "It's buried somewhere safe."

"Good place for a strongbox. Other than a bank, that is. Why's it buried?"

"It belonged to my uncle. He did some work for a bunch of men in Texas."

"Let me guess," Slocum said. "Your uncle knew some outlaws or crooked politicians or maybe even stole the money himself and squirreled it away to keep it out of reach from men like the ones that are after you now."

"You know my uncle?"

"Nope. I've just been to this dance a few times before." From what he'd seen of Jack Halsey, Slocum had a fairly good read on the man. Once again, he could thank his poker instincts as well as a strong dose of common sense for that.

When Jack spoke about his uncle, it was quickly and comfortably. "My uncle's name ain't important," he said, "but I will tell you he didn't do more than four honest days' work in his entire life. He was a crook, but he never did kill no one!"

"I never accused him of anything."

Jack nodded sternly and looked at his feet while nudging a rock with his toe. "He was the man other crooks came to when they needed to hide their money or sell stolen property. Far as anyone in the family could figure, he was taking only a sliver of a percentage from those outlaws because he never seemed to get rich."

"That's probably how he managed to stay alive and in business for more than a year," Slocum pointed out.

"That's what we thought. He was an affable sort, too. Could charm a nun right out of her habit if he was so inclined. As it turned out, he was actually shaving off a little more of that money for himself and hiding it away."

"He stole from outlaws?"

"Yep," Jack replied. "Don't know when it started, but he took a little here and a little there. He only told me about it once, and I still don't fully understand the details of how he got paid or how he explained it to the men whose money it was. Something about making them believe he was paying out fake bribes or telling someone else about taxes or some other sort of fee that had to be paid which he never paid."

Slocum chuckled. "Making up excuses to be fed to the men who were expecting their money to explain why there was a little less than what they'd been expecting. Not too bad if you can convince dangerous men that those fees are legitimate."

"Well, if anyone could do that, it was my uncle. Nobody in the family asked about who gave him the money and he never seemed to have much of it anyway, so he was just another black sheep and we all went about our business. Then my uncle died."

"How did he die?"

"What's that matter?" Jack snapped.

"For a man in your uncle's line of work, there's a wide spectrum of ways he could meet his end. If it wasn't as simple as breaking his neck when falling off his horse, that could mean someone found out what he'd been doing with that money over all those years. And considering our predicament of late, the men who discovered your uncle's scam could very well be the ones that are out there looking to put you in their sights."

"I suppose you got a point there."

Obviously, Jack missed his uncle. Without dwelling on the morbid details, Slocum said, "So . . . the key?"

"Before my uncle died, he sent a letter telling me that if anything happened to him, I should go to a bank in Dallas and pick up another letter he left with a teller there. He died soon after, I went to Dallas, and there was the letter along with some money and that key. The second letter said there was a strongbox and that it was buried . . . well . . . it told me where it was buried and that I should take the money to divvy it out to the rest of the family. He said we shouldn't make it common knowledge that we have it. Knowin' my uncle the way me and my whole family does, we guessed where it came from. Since we ain't exactly rich ourselves, it was not the time to start asking questions.

"I rode out to get to the strongbox when one of Oklahoma Bill's gang found me and started chasing me across the whole damn state. Lucky for me, you and that sheriff found

Oklahoma Bill. I continued along my way, made camp, and was attacked by those goddamn wolves. You know the rest of the story."

"Sure I do. There's only one piece I'm still missing."

Jack sighed and kicked the rock he'd been nudging hard enough to send it sailing into the woods. "You want to know why I lied to you about the ring and all?"

"That's the piece."

"Because I could tell you weren't the sort of man who'd be all fired up to help someone like me claim a bunch of money stolen by a disreputable uncle. There was all that talk about you ridin' on that posse and the doctor trying to get you to sign on as a deputy. Still, I'm a fairly good judge of character, and it seemed like you weren't ready to settle in Rocas Rojas. I needed someone to help me get that key. I inherited some of my uncle's fast-talking skills, so I thought I could get you to take the job. Now that you know the truth, I'm guessing you're ready to ride off and leave me at the mercy of these savages?"

Slocum dropped his cigar on the ground and crushed it beneath his boot. He then turned to Jack and said, "Maybe you're not as good at judging character as you think."

"So you wanna shoot me here and now?" Jack asked with a wince.

"All right. You're a downright terrible judge of character. I may want to shoot you, but I'm not going to. At least not right this instant. As far as your uncle's money goes, I'd say he pulled off one hell of a trick to steal from thieves for as long as he did. One thing you should learn from him, though, is that deeds like that never fail to come back to bite you on the ass."

"There was something to that effect in his letter."

"Sounds to me like the men your uncle stole from were involved in fairly big jobs."

"How do you know that?"

"Small jobs give robbers small amounts of money. It's

the kind of thing that they could just divvy up afterward or stick under a mattress for a while. Larger amounts need to be socked away with a little more efficiency. Either that or he worked with gangs that didn't trust each other enough to split up the take themselves. Either way, I'd say your uncle was sitting on money taken from banks and payrolls and such."

According to the puzzled expression on Jack's face, that was all news to him. Since he'd just been thinking aloud, Slocum didn't bother explaining any further. "I only bring it up because a lot of that money was probably already written off by whoever lost it. Your uncle's sliver that he took wasn't much of the pie and even less of it was put into that strongbox, so I don't have any qualms with taking a piece for myself."

"Oh," Jack said, obviously disappointed in the fact that all of that talk ended up with his money still being taken. "I guess that's something."

"It means you had no reason to lie to me. More importantly, it means I'll hold up my end of our arrangement."

Now that did brighten his features. "You won't leave me with these savages?"

"No. But you might want to do yourself a real big favor while you're here."

"What's that, John?"

"Stop calling them savages."

17

Dan, Young, and Karl worked their way along the Potrillos at a steady, deliberate pace. They weren't about to let Jack slip through their fingers again. The three gunmen took turns at the front, where they could look for anything that might let them know they were still on the right trail. Once Slocum and Jack had met up with the larger group of horses, tracking them became even easier.

It didn't take long for Dan to figure out the other group was made up of Indians. Compared to the shoes worn by other men's horses or even the way in which those horses were ridden, an Indian stood out well enough. Judging by how easily many of those tracks blended with the environment or strayed from well-worn trails, Dan guessed the Indians were Apache. He'd done enough work hunting them for the Army or anyone else willing to pay for scalps to track the sons of bitches.

The trail went cold on higher terrain, but Dan picked it up again and followed it to a spot where there had been one hell of a fight. The three outlaws stopped there long enough to give their horses a rest, which allowed Karl to pick up the tracks leading away from all those bloodstained rocks, broken arrows, and bullet casings.

After that, the trail dwindled down to almost nothing. After a bit of searching, Dan motioned for the others to halt.

"I think I found something headed that way," Karl said while waving to the east.

"You think or you know?" Dan asked.

"What difference does it make?"

"Because Halsey and Slocum are with a bunch of Apache. I'm sure of that now. They took some losses back at that spot where the fight was. Maybe even wound up with a few dead. That means they're not anxious to get hit again and are probably watching for anyone trying to come along to finish them off. When Apache get wounded in a fight, it makes 'em worse than an animal that's backed into a corner."

"You don't know they was Apache," Karl scoffed.

"How many Apache have you hunted? How many have you killed?"

The squat man shut his mouth and pursed his lips, which made his head look even more disproportionately larger than a normal person's.

"That's what I thought," Dan snarled. "Unless you got somethin' useful to say, I don't wanna hear another fucking word outta you. Understand?"

Following his orders to the letter, Karl merely nodded.

"What have you found?" Dan asked the other member of his group.

Young slid his hat back and gazed up at a darkening sky. "Not a lot and we'll be able to find even less once the sun goes down. Think I may have seen some chips on those rocks that could mean a horse or two rode up into the mountains a ways. Can't see much more from here."

Dan looked up in that direction and nodded. "Apache tend to go for higher ground when they can."

"Makes sense for just about anyone," Karl said. When

Dan looked over at him, the big fellow flinched like a scalded pup.

"Yes it does," Dan replied, granting that Karl's statement was worthy enough to go unpunished. "They've been cautious for several miles, so they could have sent some scouts up there to get a look at the terrain behind them. Or maybe they were looking for something else."

"Like what?" Young asked.

Shifting in his saddle and closing his eyes to sort through his thoughts as the cooling air of an approaching desert night washed across his face, Dan said, "Like maybe they weren't scouts as such, but guards."

"What difference does that make?"

Before Dan could step in to put the bigger fellow back into his place, Young told him, "Scouts are looking for someone or watching a bunch of riders on the move. Guards are protecting something or someone that's staying put."

"Or a whole lot of someones," Dan added.

"Like a camp?" Karl asked.

This time when Dan looked at the squat fellow, he seemed even less inclined to take a swing at him. "That's right. Just like a camp. Those Apache had to come from somewhere, right? These mountains are the perfect spot for a bunch of Indians to set up shop and squat for a while. I recall a few tribes making their home in these parts at one time or another over the years."

"You think you know where the camp is?" Young asked.

"Not as such, but I say we pick up the trail that comes down from that ridge and take it as far as we can until it gets too dark to see. First light comes, we keep going until we either catch up with that prick who's got our money or get a look at where they're holed up."

The warning he'd been given to keep his mouth shut didn't last long because Karl licked his chops excitedly when he said, "These mountains also make a good spot to bury a strongbox. There's any number of spots where old man Halsey could have stuck it. Under some rocks, in a hole, in a cave . . ."

"You mean a cave like the one we found outside of Rocas Rojas?" Young asked.

"Hey!" the squat man with the big head wailed. "I wasn't the one who kept riding before searching that spot as best we could!"

"The money wasn't there," Dan said. "If it was, Jack would have already parted ways with Slocum. Leastways, he wouldn't have taken a ride through Apache country afterward. No, Halsey's in them mountains. I'd stake my life on that."

"You got anything more than a notion to back that up?"

"When me and Bill hit that Western Union stagecoach two years back, we brought the money to Diamondback Halsey in a little shack less than a day's ride from here."

"What?" Young bellowed. "Why the hell didn't we just go to that damn shack to start with?"

"Because me and Bill tried going back there last spring and couldn't even find the damn place. Besides that, the old man was a wily old cuss and never met us in the same spot twice in a row. Never met anyone in the same spot twice. That's how come nobody ever found the bastard and took him for all he was worth during the sixteen years he was in business." Dan shook his head and smiled as if mulling over a batch of fond memories. "He was a crafty one."

"Still got caught," Karl pointed out.

"It took five or six years of him working with every gang south of the Mason-Dixon Line before anyone even got suspicious that he was doing anything more than watching over saddlebags or sacks full of stolen gold until the men who stole it could stop running or got out of jail long enough to claim it. Even when they got suspicious, nobody could prove a damn thing until the very end."

"You don't sound too upset by all of that," Young said.

Dan shrugged and allowed his face to revert back into its normal, gruff demeanor. "Thieves stealing from thieves ain't exactly new. I wouldn't expect any less. And just because we're one step closer to getting our hands on that cash don't mean we're about to ride into greener pastures. Word spreads about Diamondback Halsey's stash and there'll be blood in the water. Lots of men will lay claim to that money and most of 'em have every right. That's why we got to get to it, and now's not the time to slip up."

"You think this'll get messy?" Karl asked.

Young nodded once. "It'll get bloody as hell."

Dan pointed his horse toward the ridge that had been singled out and snapped his reins. "Wouldn't expect any less."

18

There was even more to the feast than Slocum could have hoped. After spending the better part of two days being sustained by trail rations of dried oats and jerked meat washed down by gritty coffee, the food prepared by the Apache women was above and beyond his wildest expectations. After a while, he stopped asking what the food was and just handed his appetite over to his instincts. If it smelled good, he tried some. If he liked it, he ate some more. There were things that were familiar and a few that were new to him. There was even a strange kind of sausage that Slocum had never seen in a meal prepared by any Indian tribe. It was good, though, so he ate it.

As the night wore on, the fire was stoked to cast longer shadows of the Apache dancing around it. Their singing lasted for hours. When one set of throats became tired, another set took its place. By the end of the night, every member of the tribe had taken their turn dancing. Every time Nitika was drawn into the circle, Slocum was there to watch.

She had a warm, often hesitant smile. Nitika was bashful whenever the festivities singled her out, but there was no reason for her to be hesitant. Her long tunic clung to her in just the right way for Slocum to get an idea of the curves beneath it. Her hair swayed around a perfectly rounded face, and more often than not, her dark, amber-colored eyes drifted toward him. Even when the sky had become inky black and the stars shone like polished gems, the dancing continued. Resisting the many hands that tried to keep her in the circle of dancers, she pulled away and walked over to Slocum.

He stood and reflexively reached out to hold on to her as she staggered too close to the log upon which he sat. "Watch yourself," he said. "Wouldn't want you to get hurt."

Undoubtedly, she knew every inch of the camp by memory. When Slocum's hands drifted to her waist, she allowed herself to fall another half-step toward him before placing her hands upon his chest. She lingered there, looked into his eyes, and then turned away so she could settle into a seated position. "I feel drunk. It's been a long day."

"If you'd like to make it official, I think Jack was passing around a bottle of whiskey."

"Imala has probably taken him away. She's had her eye on him."

"I suppose his tall tales have to work on someone," Slocum said.

"Maybe he is thanking her."

"For what?"

Nitika blinked and said, "I thought you would have known already. She's the one who found his key."

"What?"

She smiled again. The expression was becoming warmer and more familiar as she spent more time with him. "Did you have any of the sausage she made?"

"I did. It was delicious."

"Imala was raised on a farm by a German family before she was reunited with her tribe. It's a long story, but she learned to cook and has brought some of her adopted mother's teachings to our tribe, where she blends it with those of her own people. On special occasions, she makes something from her upbringing like that sausage. Do you know how sausage is made?"

"I know it's not pretty," Slocum joked.

"She uses an animal's stomach to hold it together. Her mother used sheep's stomach or one from a pig. Maybe also a cow."

"And that's why I don't ask about where my food comes from. Seems much better when it just shows up on my plate." The attempt to make her laugh was a reflex, but when Slocum thought more about what she was saying, it sank in. "Wait a second. So are those sausages made from the wolves?"

Nitika nodded. "Cha'to's pelt will be a prize given to our tribe's greatest hunter. The pelts of the other wolves as well as the teeth and bones will be used to make our finest weapons and aid in Ilesh's medicines, but Imala was the first one to claim Cha'to's innards. She cleaned out his stomach and found the key."

Thinking back to how the key had glistened wetly in Ilesh's hand, Slocum couldn't help shuddering. "Was Jack told all of that?"

"I don't know," she replied while looking around at the darkened camp. "Perhaps I could ask Imala. I can't seem to find her, though."

"From the way those two have been mooning over each other all night, I have a good idea what they're doing."

Nitika smiled and shifted her attention back to Slocum. "I think I do, too."

When she lowered her face, Slocum reached out to place his finger beneath her chin so he could guide it up again. "You're beautiful," he told her.

"No I'm not."

"Do you stare at yourself every day?"

"No," she replied.

"Do you have pictures taken or get someone to draw you so you can see your face whenever you please?"

"No!"

"Then you don't look at yourself enough to argue with me," he said. "I'm looking at you right now just as I have been all night long, and I'm telling you you're beautiful. If you want to dispute that, you'll need to come up with something better than a shake of your head."

She started to shake her head anyway, but caught herself and stopped so she could look directly into his eyes and say, "Thank you."

"I've heard stories about some tribes where the hunters get their pick of any woman they want."

"Have you?"

He nodded. "They get the prettiest women along with the most food and the best horses."

"Those sound like good tribes . . . if you are a hunter."

"I brought down the mighty Cha'to," Slocum said. "Does that mean I get my pick of the prettiest woman in the tribe?"

Leaning forward so her breath warmed his mouth when she spoke to him, Nitika whispered, "That is not our way, and if it was, you aren't a part of the tribe."

"Damn," he said while leaning in a little closer.

"Also," she said while angling her face just enough to brush her lips against his, "Snake Catcher was the one who killed Cha'to."

"I helped."

"And in all those stories you heard about other tribes, what did helping get those other hunters?"

Rather than continue the banter, Slocum leaned in that extra fraction of an inch to press his lips against Nitika's. She responded warmly and then pulled away. She didn't cast an eye in any other direction, but was obviously more aware of her surroundings when she got to her feet. "I think I should go," she told him.

"Long day?"

"Yes. Sleep well, John Slocum. I think you are a fine hunter." With that, she turned her back to him and crossed the camp to some of the smaller tents on the outskirts.

Slocum sat still for a few seconds as the rest of the camp continued to sing, dance, and make merry all around him. The Apache's voices weren't exactly loud, but were unrelenting as they were raised up to the starry sky amid the rhythmic beats of a pair of drummers as well as another old woman who shook a long stick with beads, teeth, and feathers tied to it to make an exotic rattling sound. Whenever he met another set of eyes, Slocum received a greeting and the occasional nodding wave. A few children were still running about, and he waded through them as he crossed the camp.

Every step took Slocum farther from the fire's warm glow. The night was crisp and the Apache songs drifted like smoke upon the cool air. Nitika was nowhere to be found, but he continued walking in the direction she'd gone. Once again allowing himself to be guided by instinct, he made his way to the camp's perimeter. Upon hearing rustling from within one of the tents, he dropped to one knee so he could pull aside the flap to get a quick look inside. That was all he needed to see Nitika lying beneath a furry blanket made from several smaller pelts that had been stitched together. Before he could ask for permission to go any farther, she pulled aside the blanket to reveal her naked body to him.

Slocum crawled inside, pulled his shirt off, unbuckled his pants, stripped out of the rest of his clothes, and kicked off his boots so he could join her on a woven mat covering the ground beneath the tent. She laughed softly at how quickly he'd undressed and lowered the animal skins on top of them both.

"Maybe the hunter should get a reward," she whispered while draping her leg over him and running a hand along his naked chest.

"Sounds fair to me." Sliding his leg between hers, Slocum

wrapped his arms around her and pulled Nitika close while kissing her on the mouth. Their passion built its own momentum and soon their probing tongues found each other.

Although she'd been timid earlier, Nitika was nothing of the sort any longer. Her hands pressed solidly against him to push Slocum onto his back so she could straddle him. She kissed him hungrily for another minute or two and then moved her mouth farther down. First she licked his neck, then she took gentle bites along his chest and stomach as her hands rubbed against his bare skin. Slocum leaned back and slid his fingers through her long, thick hair as she lowered her mouth onto his erect penis and began sucking him.

When he looked down, he could just see the outline of her shoulders and bobbing head in the bit of light cast against the surface of the tent. Her mouth made wet sucking sounds as she feasted upon him, and her tongue rubbed up and down along the bottom of his shaft. When she lingered in a certain spot, Slocum held her there so she could continue to lick and tease him. Nitika brought him right to the brink and then slowed down. When his hands moved away from the back of her head, she straightened up so the blanket fell around her.

After stroking him to keep his cock good and stiff, she crawled like a cat that was about to try and slip beneath the bottom edge of the tent. Nitika stretched her arms forward, arched her rump into the air, and looked over her shoulder at him. Slocum got to his knees and settled in behind her, admiring the sight of her round hips and thickly muscled thighs. Her skin seemed even darker in the shadows and was smooth as silk when he took her in his hands. His cock ached to be inside her, but he took his time in guiding it between her legs. By the time the tip brushed against the wet lips of her pussy, Nitika was clawing at the ground and shifting back to feel more of him. Slocum obliged by guiding his rigid member to where it needed to be and burying it inside her.

She moaned softly, moving her head slowly back and forth to toss her hair while he pumped into her. Outside, the pounding of the drums accompanied Slocum pounding his rigid pole between her moistened thighs. He placed one hand upon the supple curve at the base of her spine while reaching forward to place his other hand on her shoulder. That way, he could grip her tightly while he drove into her even harder. She braced herself against every impact, grunting as the pleasure mounted and grinding her hips against him whenever he took a moment to catch his breath.

Nitika tossed her head back and whispered in her own language. The only thing Slocum could understand was his own name. When she pressed back against him to drive his erection even deeper between her legs, Slocum grabbed her hair. Nitika pulled in a sharp, excited breath as he pulled just enough to take up the slack while pumping into her from behind. He let go only to reach around with both hands to cup her large, swaying breasts.

Her large nipples became rigid against his fingers and palms. Slocum caressed them while slowly driving into her and then eased his hands along her sides. When the mood struck him, he pulled out of her and positioned Nitika so she was lying on her back with the thick blanket spread beneath her. She opened her legs, propped herself up using her elbows, and closed her eyes in expectation of what was about to happen. Once he guided himself into her again, she let out a trembling breath and allowed her head to swing lazily from side to side.

Slocum knelt between her legs, reached down to cup her buttocks in his hands, and lifted her so he could bury his cock into her as deep as it could possibly go. He didn't have to do that for long before Nitika placed her feet upon the ground and held her hips in position so he could move his hands once more along her hips and sides while sliding in and out of her.

The lips between her legs were slick and allowed every

inch of his rigid cock to glide between them. Nitika clawed at the ground and stifled the impulse to scream as her orgasm swept through her entire body. Slocum grabbed her hips and wasn't about to let go. Her body felt warm and smooth. Her skin glistened with the sweat from their lovemaking, and her hair was a wild, tousled mess around her beautiful face. Every time he pounded into her, Nitika's breasts shook with the impact. Her stomach rose and fell with increasingly heavy breaths, and her eyes clenched shut as she was taken once more into a powerful climax.

When his own time came, Slocum leaned back and savored every moment. He could feel her thighs tensing around him with every one of her trembling breaths. After pulling out of her so he could collapse, Slocum swore he could feel everything from the soft fur of the blanket all the way to the subtle texture of smoke drifting on the night breeze.

They fell asleep right there, naked and entwined in each other's limbs. Somewhere along the line, Nitika pulled the blanket over them, but Slocum was too spent to notice.

19

Slocum was jostled awake by a familiar, insistent hand.

"John, get up."

He recognized her voice, but it took a moment for its urgency to register.

"John," Nitika hissed. "Wake up. Please!"

"Yeah. What is it?"

But he didn't have to hear her reply to know what had alarmed her. Outside, horses rumbled away from the camp and Apache voices were raised in alarm. Gunshots cracked in the distance, but were still much too close for comfort.

"Who's out there?" he asked while scrambling for his clothes, boots, and gun belt. "Are the hunters chasing someone down?"

She was naked and too shaken up to bother with looking for her tunic. "I heard the war cries and shots. I don't know what's happening."

It wasn't long before Slocum was dressed and pulling aside the flap of the tent. Outside, the sun had just made a dent in the thick gloom of early morning, and the air was cold enough to lance through his bones. "Is there anywhere safer you can go?" he asked.

"My tribe will find me if I need to hide."

"Then sit tight and be ready to move. Promise me if any of this fighting gets closer, you get with the others as quick as you can."

She nodded and pulled on her clothes. If she was like many of the other women Slocum had known, he would have worried more about her. But she was Apache and her tribe had more than likely been rousted from their sleep by gunshots more than once before.

Slocum stepped out and crossed the middle of the camp toward the sounds of battle. "Jack?"

Hobbling in boots that still hadn't been pulled all the way over his feet and wrapped in a shirt that was closed by buttons stuffed through the wrong holes, Jack Halsey fidgeted with the buckle of his gun belt while making his way to the corral. He glanced over with a fearful twitch at the sound of his own name. When he saw Slocum, every muscle in his face relaxed. "Oh, it's you, John! Thank God!"

"What did you do?"

"Huh?"

"What the hell is happening out here? Did you try to make off with that key?"

"Now there's a fine how-do-you-do!" Behind Jack, Imala pulled on some clothes to cover her ample bosom as she emerged from another one of the tents on the periphery of the camp.

"So where is the key?" Slocum asked.

"I don't know, but—"

"Ilesh," Imala said. She emerged from the tent a little farther, but pulled her head back in when another wave of gunshots crackled outside of camp. "Ilesh has your key, but I think Chief Gopan can get it for you."

"If that's the case, you should be able to get ahold of it," Slocum said. "Hand it over to Jack and we'll be on our way."

"To Jack?" she asked.

Slocum nodded. "That's right. It's his key. Cha'to took it from him when he took his fingers."

Despite the growing amount of chaos inside and away from the camp, Imala's face beamed with admiration. "So what you told me was true? You rode after Cha'to to reclaim your prize?"

"Of course it's true!" Jack said. "Why does everyone think I'm some kind of damn liar?"

Rather than point out a few obvious reasons, Slocum allowed the other man to play his part so Imala could follow through with hers. Slocum couldn't blame the other man for bending the truth to impress a woman. If Jack was going to be held accountable for something like that, then damn near every man on earth would have some explaining to do. "Just go get that key," he said. "I'll help with whatever's going on out there."

Jack blinked as if in a daze when he asked, "You'd do that for me?"

"It's what you're paying me for, isn't it? Just keep this gratefulness in mind when we're splitting up that money you aim to dig up."

"You can count on it, John! Jack Halsey is a man who repays his debts. You'll get a portion of my uncle's fortune! I can guarantee it!"

"Just shut your damn mouth and get moving!"

Jack nodded fiercely and surprised Slocum again by rushing over to Imala to shield her with his body as he escorted her to the largest teepee in the camp.

From there, Slocum hurried to the space roped off as a corral. Although his horse and gear were right where he'd left them, the saddle was still on the ground, where it would do him the least amount of good. At least his Winchester was still lying beneath the rest of his rig. He grabbed the rifle, checked to make sure it was loaded, and then decided to run toward the commotion on foot instead of taking the time to mount his horse. The gunshots were closer than he'd guessed, which meant the shooters were closing in on the camp.

Slocum headed for a ridge of rock on the northern border of the camp and scrambled for higher ground. He made it less than halfway before a sharp voice made his trigger finger twitch.

"Are these the men Jack Halsey spoke about?" Snake Catcher asked from atop the ridge. Even though Slocum had been looking up there to see where he'd wanted to go and had glanced up several times while making his ascent, he'd completely missed the Apache, who lay like just another stone overlooking the camp.

"Don't know yet," Slocum said.

The Apache stretched his arm down to offer Slocum a hand in climbing the rest of the way up. The ridge wasn't very tall, but allowed them to gaze down at the gulley sloping away from them. As soon as he was up there, Slocum could see the men who had taken position behind some trees about sixty yards away. After all that had happened in the time since they'd left Rocas Rojas, Slocum had nearly forgotten the faces of the men who'd come into town in search of him and Jack. Seeing them again, however, brought those memories rushing back. "Yep," he said. "That's them."

"Our scouts found them just before sunrise," Snake Catcher explained. "One of those men started shooting and they've been drawing in like a noose. They killed one of my warriors and wounded another." His mouth curled into a scowl that was filled with equal parts anger and disgust. "Shot the first one in the back and wounded the other for no reason."

"They got reason, all right. How many men do you have left?"

"Flying Spear and one other are the only ones other than me that are able-bodied. The wounded braves remain behind to protect the elders, women, and children."

"Some of those men could barely walk," Slocum said as he thought about the damage that had been done to the hunting party. "And how many are still feeling headaches from last night's party?"

Snake Catcher didn't answer, but obviously wasn't pleased with what came to mind.

Slocum slithered on his belly all the way to the edge of the ridge. As he sighted along the top of his barrel, he was able to pick out the sources of the shots. "I only see two of them. Is that all there is?"

"I don't know. The shooting just started."

And then it all snapped into focus. Slocum knew what was going on, and all he had to do was utilize an old Indian saying that told him the best way to know a man was to walk a mile in his moccasins. Without hesitating long enough to second-guess himself, Slocum stood up and waved his hat in the air while shouting, "Hey, assholes! Remember me?"

The two gunmen in the trees below poked their heads out for a moment and shifted their aim to the top of the ridge. Slocum dropped down hard enough to knock some of the wind from his lungs, which didn't keep him from rolling onto his belly so he could once again rest the Winchester upon the rocks in front of him.

"What are you doing?" Snake Catcher asked. "I need them to stay still long enough for me to attack from the side."

Shots hissed inches above Slocum's head. He fired once in the general direction of the trees, which was intended only to give him enough breathing room to aim the next round. "I know what I'm doing," he said to the angry Apache.

"It was foolish for me to hunt with a white man. You know only how to pull a trigger."

"That's right," Slocum replied as he fired again. One shot punched through a tree being used by one of the gunmen for cover and the next clipped the man who hopped away from the spot that had just been targeted. It wasn't a killing blow, but enough to quiet that shooter down for a moment or two. "Keep that shooting business in mind because that's what's gonna help us catch some real big snakes."

The Apache wasn't in good humor at the start, and hearing the play of words involving his name didn't help matters.

Karl groaned after being clipped by the Winchester's bullet, tried to stay on his feet, wobbled, and then fell over like a sack of potatoes. "God damn!" he wailed when his backside hit the rocky soil.

Taking a moment to reload his Sharps rifle, Young glanced down at the larger man and said, "I told you to stay behind cover."

"That round cut through this tree like it was butter! What the hell do you expect me to do?"

"Stick yer nose out like a damned fool! That makes perfect sense."

"That's John Slocum up on that ridge. I seen him with my own eyes."

"Now all we gotta do is to kill him," Young said as he dropped to one knee so he could fire up at the ridge. "We take him out first and then all we got to deal with is a bunch of wounded, drunken Indians. From all the blood we found, I'd wager these that came out to greet us now are the only men we got to worry about." He fired and then quickly picked out a different target. The Apache who had been approaching from the west had made it to within six paces of the outlaws, but stood up to charge when he knew he'd been spotted. He made it halfway to Young's position and was stopped dead by a bullet that hit him squarely in the chest. Still bringing his rifle around, Young looked back at his partner and said, "Much obliged."

Karl held his smoking .44 in a steady hand when something behind him hissed. His head snapped forward and his eyes rolled up into their sockets. After a quiet moment, the bigger man slumped over to reveal the arrow sticking out of the back of his skull.

"God damn savages!" Young shouted as he pivoted around with the rifle braced against his shoulder. More shots continued to rain down from the ridge, but he was more interested in the solitary figure hunched over a stump while notching another arrow into his bow. Young sighted along the top of his Sharps and fired. The Apache archer yelped and was spun to the side by the impact of the bullet. Before he could fall, Young put another round into him. The Apache hit the ground in a heap and didn't move again.

A piercing whistle sounded from the top of the ridge to catch Young's attention. The rifleman fired toward Slocum's silhouette, only to kick up sparks as the bullet chipped some rocks. Something rustled behind him and the only thing Young saw when he turned around was the angry snarl on Flying Spear's face as the Apache rushed at him with his tomahawk in hand.

Jack and Imala stood in the chief's teepee as Gopan rooted through a small pouch. "Hurry up and hand over that key," Jack said urgently. "We don't have all day!"

Imala hissed a warning at him in her own tongue. Jack didn't need to understand the woman's language to know she didn't appreciate anyone speaking to the chief of her people like that. Although Jack bit his tongue, he stuck out his hand and shook it impatiently as if that would make the key appear in his grasp any faster.

"That's right, old man," Dan said as he stepped into the teepee and drew the flap shut behind him. "We are in a bit of a rush." He already had his pistol drawn and pointed so he could hit Jack or either of the two Apache with the same amount of effort. "And don't waste a thought on what Slocum's doing. Him and the rest of the redskins will be too busy slaughtering the boys I brought along with me. I'm guessing my men will thin out your herd, too," he said to the chief, "so you might as well hand over the key."

Gopan turned the pouch over so the key fell heavily to the ground. He then stood and glared silently at the outlaw without making another move.

"Kick it over," Dan said.

The chief remained as still as a boulder. He didn't even flinch when Dan pulled his trigger to put a round through his heart. Gopan silently fell.

"I'm in a hurry," Dan snarled. "Since you folks ain't feeling cooperative, I'll do my own damn work." He started moving toward the spot where the key had landed, but couldn't take half a step before he was stopped by a grip that tightened around his shoulder and pulled him back toward the tent's entrance.

"Drop the gun," Slocum snarled from directly behind the outlaw.

Dan couldn't move more than a fraction of an inch in any direction because of the arm that had snaked around his neck from behind. As the grip cinched in tight enough to cut the flow of blood through the arteries on either side of his throat, Dan allowed his gun arm to dangle at his side.

Pressing the barrel of his Schofield even harder into the outlaw's backbone, Slocum growled, "I said drop it!"

Still hanging on to his pistol, Dan smirked while eyeing the key on the ground in front of him. "I know the sort of man you are, Slocum. You ain't about to shoot someone in the back after you already got the drop on him."

"And you're the sort of man who throws his own partners to the wolves just to distract these Apache long enough for you to sneak in and gun down an unarmed old man."

"Yeah, but that's me. Not you."

Jack knew Slocum well enough to become increasingly uncomfortable with the standoff that had developed.

"Maybe you're right," Slocum said. Then, he shoved Dan farther into the teepee while spinning him around.

The outlaw stopped just shy of tripping over the circle of

rocks that had contained the previous night's fire, grabbed for the key, and snapped his arm up to put his gun to work.

Slocum fired from the hip. His eyes had been fixed so intently on his target that there wasn't a doubt in his mind he would hit it. Dan took half a step back, coughed up some blood, and kept struggling to raise his gun. When it seemed as if the outlaw might actually dredge up enough strength to pull his trigger, Slocum put him down with as much ceremony as he would have killed a rabid dog. In the end, that was all the murdering son of a bitch deserved.

By the time Slocum had taken away Dan's pistol and Jack reclaimed his key, Ilesh peeked inside the teepee to ask, "Is it safe to come in?"

Imala rushed over to the shaman with tears streaming down her face as she explained what happened in a sobbing rush. Slocum told him, "He was shot before I could get here. I'm sorry."

"Did he die like a warrior?" Snake Catcher asked as he moved past the elder. He still wore Slocum's hat after putting it on to distract Dan's boys, but when he saw the chief's body, he couldn't take it off fast enough.

"Damn near spat his last breath into his killer's face," Slocum said.

Ilesh nodded solemnly. "Then there is no reason to be sorry."

Looking at Snake Catcher, Slocum asked, "I take it you passed for me up on that ridge long enough to get the job done?"

Snake Catcher knelt beside his chief and spoke in a voice that was drawn tighter than a bowstring. "The other two white men are dead. Flying Spear and one of the wounded scouts rode out to make sure no more are coming."

"That's a good idea. Your tribe might want to find a new camp, all the same."

The shaman nodded. "Yes. Too much blood has been spilled here for no good reason. You stood tall to protect us,

•

John Slocum, but I will still ask you and Jack Halsey to leave."

Slocum nodded respectfully. "I understand." He placed his hat upon his head and said, "We'll go. There's just one thing I ask as a favor."

"You have done much for my people," Snake Catcher told him. "If there is something I can do for you, tell me what it is."

"That gray wolf that was killed," Slocum replied. "Did you bring it back to the camp?"

"Yes."

"I could use a piece of its hide."

"Take the whole thing," Snake Catcher told him. "Wear it with pride."

"I will, but that old dog is going to be more use than that."

20

The stretch of land was a lonely tract of sand-blasted clay on the bank of a dried-up riverbed six miles north of the Mexican border. Jack insisted there had been water flowing past the old graveyard the last time he'd seen it, but there wasn't even a hint of it now. After passing the bleached wooden crosses leaning in the battered patch of earth where they'd been planted, the two men rode for another quarter mile and then came to a stop.

Since he was the one to signal for them to halt, Jack was first to climb down from his horse. "This is it!" he said anxiously. "I can feel it!"

"That's what you said about the last two places we stopped," Slocum groaned.

"And you accuse *me* of bellyaching. This is the place. The last one was just a graveyard. The one before that was a riverbed with part of a graveyard nearby."

"There were some twigs stuck in the dirt at odd angles. They weren't markers and that wasn't a damn graveyard."

180

"Well, what we just passed is a graveyard and this," Jack said while pointing down to a spot where the ground had been smoothed out by a stream that was as dead as the men planted in the distance, "is the spot my uncle used to take me to catch lizards."

"Then get to digging."

As Jack hunkered down and used a small shovel to chip away at the scorched ground, two riders thundered through the graveyard without the slightest bit of respect shown to those who still rested there. Without looking up from what he was doing, Jack asked, "They still following us?"

"Yep."

"Want me to lend a hand when they get here?"

"Just be ready and for the love of all that's holy . . ."

"I know, I know. I'll keep my damn mouth shut."

Slocum stood his ground as the two men rode toward him. One of them drew his horse to a stop about fifty yards away while the other kept coming until he was close enough for Slocum to see the sweat glistening off of his smooth, olive-colored skin.

"I'm Salvatore Majesco," the Italian man announced.

"What's that to me?"

"Nothing, Mr. Slocum, but I imagine the name may mean something to the nephew of Diamondback Halsey."

"Diamondback?" Slocum asked as he cast half a glance at Jack. "Was your uncle dangerous enough to be named after a rattler?"

When Jack didn't respond, Salvatore explained, "Not hardly. One of his first jobs looking after stolen property was for a gang that stole a shipment of diamonds from a safe in San Antonio. The law as well as a few bounty hunters tried to locate the gems while the gang was in prison. When he was released, the gang's leader said that Halsey sat on the diamonds so well for so long that they must have become lodged up his . . . well . . . I'm sure you see where that is headed."

"Yeah," Slocum said. "I see. What is it you want from us that's important enough for you to have been dogging our tails for three days?"

"I was one of Diamondback's last clients. Whatever money you are trying to claim rightfully belongs to me."

"We don't even know if this is the spot."

"Mr. Halsey seems fairly excited," Salvatore said. "He's convinced this is the spot."

"Jack gets excited about a lot of things. Why don't you men mosey along and leave us alone? Diamondback is dead, and whatever you did to earn the money you gave him, I'm sure it doesn't entitle you to a piece of whatever he's worth now that he's gone. Easy come, easy go, right?"

Salvatore's face was cordial without being friendly. "No, Mr. Slocum," he said through a snakelike smile. "I went through a lot of trouble to get here. I will most definitely not easily go."

"How'd you even know about my inheritance?" Jack asked.

"At the end of his life, your uncle became very sloppy," the Italian explained. "That is what got him killed. Many of his customers found out about what he stole, but none of them thought it was worth the trouble of coming to claim it."

"And you're different, huh?" Nodding toward the man who still sat fifty yards away, Slocum asked, "That why you hired a bunch of gunhands to back you? Because you figured it would be worth the trouble?"

"Diamondback Halsey saw a lot of money and valuables pass through his hands," Salvatore said. "I imagine he stashed away enough to live rather comfortably."

Slocum studied the Italian carefully and made sure Salvatore knew he was doing it. "I may not be a rich man, but I seen enough of them to spot one from a mile away. In this situation, a rich man would have ridden up with at least four or five gunmen in his company. You brought one. You're not a dangerous man either, because that gun belt you're wearing is more for looks than anything else. You obviously used Jack's uncle's services quite a bit, which means you're probably a thief who didn't have the guts to face down a posse and would rather hand his ill-gotten gains to an old man instead of fighting to keep it where you can see it."

"Don't test me, Mr. Slocum."

"Or what? You'll send some killers after me? You already took your shot where that was concerned and it didn't turn out too well." Slocum reached into his jacket pocket, which caused the man in the distance to lever a round into the rifle he was carrying.

"Easy, Zack," Salvatore shouted.

Slocum went easy as well. Although the ride to that particular riverbed took longer than he'd anticipated, it had given him plenty of time to cut off a strip of the wolf's pelt the Apache had given him and shave it down so the fur looked less like an animal's coat and more like long, gray stubble sprouting from a piece of tattered skin at irregular intervals. Some cutting here, some trimming there, and the piece looked just rough enough to serve its purpose. It was a lot of trouble to go through when the Apache may have been just as happy to give him the real item, but carrying another man's scalp was a bit out of Slocum's range no matter who that man was. He tossed the strip of skin over to Salvatore and said, "That's what's left of the killers you sent after us. Had some help from the Apache, but I think I picked up enough tips to learn how to scalp a man on my own next time."

Having caught the leathery strip without knowing what to make of it, Salvatore looked down at it with wide eyes and threw it to the ground. "Jesus Christ! You scalped him?"

"According to what Jack told me, the smart money was on there being someone behind those three killers who'd hired them to chase after us. I figured whoever hired them might like to know what they got for their money. Now, unless that rifleman out there is better than all of those other gunmen combined, I'd say you should both mosey along and leave us to our business."

Salvatore looked down at the strip of hairy skin as if he were afraid it would jump up and bite his horse. He then tugged on his reins to ride back toward the graveyard. "Come on, Zack," he announced as if he was making a royal decree. "We're through here."

The rifleman stayed put until his employer rode to his side.

"You really think they'll just leave?" Jack whispered.

Slocum watched the two men converse between themselves and said, "If they had the stomach for a fair fight, they wouldn't have hired them other three in the first place."

Sure enough, Slocum watched both men ride away as Jack continued to dig. About two hours later, there were several freshly made holes in the dry ground. The final one clanged when Jack drove his shovel into it. "Found it!" he declared.

After so much anticipation, Slocum had become genuinely excited to see what the dead old-timer had left behind.

"You stuck with me through this whole thing," Jack said breathlessly while using his fingers to scrape at the dirt to reveal the edges of a dented metal container only slightly bigger than a cigar box. "I'm cutting you in for a percentage as well as your additional fee for coming all this way with me. How's five percent of what's in here sound?"

"If that's what you think is fair for getting you this far in one piece."

Glancing nervously at the discarded piece of wolf skin as if it truly were the scalp of Slocum's enemy, he said, "You're right. Ten percent's more fair. Now let's see how rich we're all gonna be!"

Slocum looked down as Jack removed the box from the dirt.

Jack's hands trembled as he tugged at the lid.

The wind blew as if Diamondback himself were there for the show.

The box opened with a grating metallic squeal and inside, in crumpled bills of various denominations, was what looked to be about two hundred and fifty dollars.

"This has gotta be a mistake," Jack said as he scooped out the cash and counted it up. "There's less than three hundred dollars here!"

"What else did your uncle do?"

"What do you mean?"

"I mean he couldn't have made a living just by taking a little percentage of the money he was hiding. There couldn't have even been many of those jobs in the course of a year."

When Jack turned the box over and shook it, a few bits of rock fell out that might have been gold. If so, that could add about twenty more dollars to the total.

"Tell you what," Slocum said. "Keep your percentage. I'll just take my fee."

"But . . ." Jack sputtered. "There was supposed to be . . . I thought . . ."

"You think this is enough to split among the rest of your family?"

"It's barely enough to pay for the expense of getting here!"

Slocum helped Jack collect his inheritance and rode with him to a hotel in the nearest town. There was always the possibility that Jack was tricking him into leaving with a minimum for payment, but he doubted that was the case. If Jack was good enough to fake what looked to be heartbroken tears at the corners of his eyes, he would have already made a fortune as an actor. As it was, he was just a poor fool with dashed hopes.

They parted ways after sharing a meal at a local steak house. The last time Slocum saw Diamondback Halsey's nephew, Jack was setting out to find Imala with hat in hand and a hundred and fourteen dollars in his pockets.

Watch for

SLOCUM AND THE TRAIL TO YELLOWSTONE

395th novel in the exciting SLOCUM series
from Jove

Coming in January!

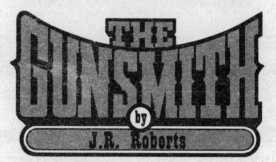